Steve

IF YOU DON'T PUSH NOTHING MOVES

*To Tammy
my BFF.
Love
Steve*

Single Action Productions

ACKNOWLEDGEMENTS

The author expresses great appreciation to Layding Lumunba Kaliba for the use of this title and his relentless support, objectivity and friendship, also Alfreda Reynolds for her insight, vitality and support.

A special thanks must also be given to the following people: Duane, Brenda, Larry and Cathy (blood will always be thicker), all of the writers from I.M.A.G.E.S Collective, my mother, sister Alberta Williams (Bread of Heaven) and most of all -Almighty God.

In the beginning and in the end, this endeavor was inspired by one man. One man who desperately and thoroughly affects, creates and molds my persona - One man who supports
                     One man who understands
                     One man who lifts my world – H. L. Williams

---

This book represents the third edition of If You Don't Push Nothing Moves. Over the past quarter century there has been many changes in my world, but none more remarkable than the birth of my second daughter, Imani. Together with Nyema, they are the dynamic duo of my life. Words could hardly encompass the symbolism of how it feels to share my life with them. This addition has been revised (particularly in pictures and design) to reflect some of the personal and societal changes in my life since its original publication.

I trust that you will enjoy this inspirational book of poems and short stories. The poems are just as compelling and thought-provoking now as they were 25 years ago - if not more.

Copyright © 1986 by Steve Williams   All Rights Reserved

No part of this book may be reproduced in any form, be it electronic or mechanical, including photocopy, recording, or any storage and retrieval system (except for purposes of review or publication) without the written permission from the author. Inquiries about the author or any part of this book should be addressed c/o the author at the address below.

Steve Williams
Georgetown, SC
424steve@gmail.com or (864) 346-0749

ISBN-13:978-1492293057,
ISBN-10:1492293059

DEDICATION

This book is dedicated to my father Herbert L. Williams, my mother Alberta Williams and my daughters, Nyema (Prosperity) and Imani (Faith)

TABLE OF CONTENTS

INTRODUCTION	07
THE NATURE OF A POET	09
TELL YOUR SONS AND DAUGHTERS	11
MORE THAN FRIENDS LESS THAN LOVERS	15
A SENSE OF OUGHTNESS	17
IT'S A BOY / MISLED	19
TERRANCE FAGAN SMILED TODAY	21
EXPECTATIONS	23
I PLEDGE	25
THE 23RD PSALMS	27
ERASE	29
ADULTHOOD	31
SANCTIMONIOUS SAUCE / MADE IT LOOK NATURAL	33
WINNER	35
WOMEN	37
IF A GIRL ISN'T PRETTY	39
HOW MANY LIES	41
SUNDAY TO BE EXACT	43
A FEW GOOD MEN	45
FINDERS-KEEPERS / SOMETHING IN THE MIRROR	47
FREE TO BE A FAMILY	49
TAKE THESE BROKEN WINGS / ANYBODY CAN	51
METAPHOR OF LIFE	53
OPEN DOOR POLICY	55
SWEET POTATO PIE	57
TELL ME TOMORROW	59
SORRY ABOUT THE CONFUSION	61
FAMILY PORTRAIT	63
AIN'T IN THE MOOD	65
CAN'T SMILE IT AWAY	67
NYEMA	69
NO CHARGE	73
YEAR OF THE CHILD	75
I UNDERSTAND	77
THE DEMISE	79
OUR FLOWERS	81
IF YOU DON'T PUSH NOTHING MOVES	83
CARDS YOU'RE DEALT	85
HATE DON'T MAKE NOISE	87
WHERE DO WE GET THE STRENGTH?	89
TONGUE IN CHEEK	91
NEVER LET A MAN HIT YOU MORE THAN ONCE	93
THIS IS A LOVE POEM	95
WHO WROTE THE RULES?	96

HOW DO WE SAY GOOD-BYE?	97
NIGHTINGALES	99
I COMMISSION YOU	101
THERE'S A RHYTHM TO LIFE / CALM DOWN	104
JUST A TESTIMONY	105
JESUS CHRIST WAS A SOCIAL WORKER	107
NO COMMENT	109
UNSUNG HEROES	110
CHAMPION	112
RUMOR – CONSUMER	113
MEMBERS ONLY / HARD TIMES FOR LOVERS	115
I WILL / AIN'T NO SUCH THING	117
MOTHER REARDON DRINKS A LITTLE	119
TOUCH BASE	121
LET THE STRONG HELP THE WEAK	123
WAIT	124
HEAVEN IS	125
TELL GOD WE NEED HIM DOWN HERE	127
NO DEPOSIT - NO RETURN	129
BE UNCOMMON	131
I ALWAYS WANTED TO BE SOMEBODY	133
WHERE DOES THE SEA END?	135
OTHER SIDE OF THE TRACKS / LOVE IS LOVE	136
PRIDE AND HUMOR	137
CONVERSATION # 1	138
NO ONE NEEDS TO FEEL INFERIOR	140
SUMMERTIME	143
I SEE THE WORLD	146
YESTERDAY'S CHILDREN	147
HARD RAIN / DISSONANCE	148
MUTUAL	149
KINDERGARTEN MEMORIES & PAINFUL REMINDERS	151
COMING INTO HIS MANHOOD	155
CUM BY Y'A	156
WHAT'S THE WORLD DOING OUT THERE?	158
TO HIM THAT WOULD BE GREAT	159
TERRITORIAL BEHAVIOR	161
STRANGE FRUIT	163
SOME FOLKS ARE THE HARDEST TO DEAL WITH	165
MILITANT	167
WHATEVER THE TOLL	169
A POEM FOR YOU	171
DREAM ENCOUNTER	173
SIMPLE SCIENCE	174
RUNNING IN THE NIGHT	178
DREAM HOUSE	183

INTRODUCTION

When I think of the title of this book, I think primarily of oppressed people in the world. I think of people who have "made it." There are some people in this world who understand meaningful words like "determination "more than they comprehend the word "handicapped." They understand "poverty and oppression" much more than "racism and discrimination." This book is for them.

Those of us who refuse to hide behind labels such as "underprivileged, race, illiterate, poor," should continue to fight the good fight and run a good race. This book is for people who are overachievers despite the odds; people, who in some cases lose their lives, but win their dignity.

Most of all, this book is for the children of the world. Children that are brave enough to withstand humiliation in the face of oppression and courageous enough to take up the struggle until the battle is won.

As I walk the streets of America, I am moved by the plight of the poor, the homeless and the disenfranchised. However, I am even more puzzled by the level of apathy for them. I understand that the so-called status quo must ultimately be maintained by whatever powers there may be. But, it is my opinion that we've reached the apex of our struggle for dignity and the visual effects of our dilemma can now be exposed.

A special thanks to Brother Layding Lumumba Kaliba (Single Action Productions) for bringing this condition to my attention and giving me the title for this book. It is particularly appropriate at this moment to shout from the highest mountain, "If you don't push - nothing moves."

                                                                          Steve Williams
                                                                              (1986)

THE NATURE OF A POET

The nature of a poet can be beautiful. It's a perspective that's overlooked by many; a unique observation that is both objective and subjective. A poet strokes expressions and images with the only tools he has - words. Riding buses or subways, watching TV, listening to radio, attending church, Sunday picnics or simply 4 AM snacks can be a productive and provocative experience for a poet.

But there's another side to many poets. It seems that many poets fall into the "tender trap." They succumb to the foolishness that theirs is the ultimate, definitive, artistic creation. They use "cute" words and charming slogans to define their anesthetic approach all the while stroking their sensitive egos. Occasionally, they use "heavy" terms such as "creative spirit" or "who am I?" and "syncopated inspirations." I never knew what any of that crap meant - do you? I guess it serves the purpose of good copy.

The nature of a poet is unfortunately for far too many of them selfish, pompous, arrogant, egotistical, cliquish and incredibly defensive. Please do not find yourself on the outside of a writer's collective or literary club looking in. Don't make the mistake of asking the question "what's the poem all about?" or inquiring, "I don't get it" to a poet.

Poets are like singers or musicians - everybody knows one personally. Everybody has a cousin or an uncle or friend who's a poet. Pound for pound they're always the "BADDEST" poets around. We should all check them out to feel where they are coming from. I guess if you accept the premise that anyone who can carry a note is a great singer, then anyone who can write a poem must be a great poet - and don't they know it!

Seriously, if the nature of a poet turns you off, then welcome to the club. I get a little sick and tired of snobbish, wordy, boring poems and their authors. Poetry is simply a forum or campus for expression. I never compare poems or poets to one another. It's senseless and narrow-minded to weigh poets on a scale when there's no uniformity in degree. How can anyone's expression be critiqued or compared to someone else's?

Poems need not be defended or super analyzed. Give me poems to feel, console, cajole, inspire and muse to. When it comes to poetry, I've got a bottom-line mentality. After all is said and done, either you like it or you don't.

TELL YOUR SONS AND DAUGHTERS

We must tell our sons and daughters who they really are

They are an unrepeatable gift to this universe
Blessed and highly favored
Born God's original and they must
never allow someone to make them over

Tell your sons and daughters
as they begin to fly high in life
there will always be those
who will attempt to stand on their wings -
but be not grounded

Tell them that someone else's opinion of them
does not have to become their reality

Let us remind our sons and daughters
to be careful of the company they keep
because who you run with says who you are
That if you run with losers
then you'll end up a loser
Birds of a feather flock together
You cannot soar like an eagle -
if you're running around with pigeons

We must tell our sons and daughters
to examine their lives
because the unexamined life
is not worth living
But in doing so, they must never
seek the counsel of an unproductive person
Rather, they must surround themselves
with people who are planted and
attempting to grow
Who are not just going through life
but growing through life
For an ounce of example
is worth a pound of advice

And in their curious years
when they begin to scratch
the inevitable itch
Let us tell our sons and daughters
that kisses aren't contracts
presents aren't promises
and sex, is a very poor substitute for love

But if somehow
one of our sons and daughters
gets knocked-up or knocked out
Let us tell our sons and daughters
that if you get knocked out in life -
try and land on your back
because if you can look up - you can get up

Tell your sons and daughters
to stay out of the fast lane
because the Bible says -
"Wide is the road which leads to destruction
and narrow the one that leads to life"
But few-there-be who will find it

Because few-there-be who understand
When we pray for strength
God sends us difficulties - which makes us strong
We ask for favors and He gives us opportunities
We pray for wisdom and He gives us problems –
the solution of which develops wisdom
We plead for courage
and He sends us dangers to overcome
We seek prosperity
and He gives us brain and brawn to work

Tell your sons and daughters
much of what they will ever get out of life
will come from eating the bread of adversity
and drinking the waters of affliction
But the genius of success is for the few-there-be

who can see their problem as a God-ordained
opportunity cleverly disguise as an obstacle
for them to rise up to meet it

Tell your sons and daughters
that anything difficult
is never going to be easy
That by the yard - it's hard
but inch by inch - anything's a cinch

Tell your sons and daughters
things may happen around them
and things may happen to them
but the only thing that matters -
is that which happens in them

As the storms of life begins to beat up
against their shores - and it will
This is not the time to lose their faith
Because faith is the oil that takes
the friction out of living

Let us tell our sons and daughters
as they began to entertain the
voices of homicide, genocide
and maybe even suicide -
that "Weeping endures for a night
but joy cometh in the morning"

Tell your sons and daughters
There is no night so long
      no mountain so high
      no valley so low
      no hurt so heavy
      no pain so great
      "That neither death, -
      nor life,

nor angels,
nor principalities,
Neither height
nor depth,
nor powers,
nor sickness
nor famine"
nor crack
nor cancer
nor family
nor sex
nor A.I.D.S
nor drugs
nor poverty
nor racism
or anything shall be able to separate
them from the love of God

Tell your sons and daughters
that in Christ Jesus
they are more than conquerors -

They are *SOMEBODY!!!*

MORE THAN FRIENDS LESS THAN LOVERS

Give me the creator
And not so much the creature
Let me see the essence of you
and keep the other features

Instead of reinforcing the
fantasies of your lust
I will attempt to love you
with a holistic thrust

Together, we can promote
the artistry of our talents
and arrest out sexuality
when it's compelled to be unbalanced

Please allow me to apologize
when I've treated you wrong
And if necessary,
oblige me a shoulder –
strong enough to cry on
Give me the means
And not so much the end

I don't so much need a lover
but I can surely use a friend

A SENSE OF OUGHT-NESS

You ought to be loved and cared for
                  comforted and feared for
with hugs and kisses throughout the day

You ought to run
You ought to play

You ought to be free to frolic
        and free to explore
        free to discover
        and free to adore

Your days should be wonderful
and your nights spectacular

Because there's a sense of ought-ness in you

You ought to have life
and have it more abundantly

You should be swingin slidin and runnin rings
                            around rosies
There ought to be a mommy *and* a daddy
in your world,
        nourishing you and
           encouraging you to- crawl and climb
                to push and pull
                or just - do you

You ought to have clothes on your back
and food on your table
Heat on cold days and cool on hot nights

Until you're able
to tell right from wrong -
EVEN YOUR WRONGS SHOULD BE RIGHT!

Because there's a sense of ought-ness in you
I see it shining through

You should be worry-free
with no one holding you back
You ought not concern yourself
with what you don't know

There shouldn't be any labels of blue for boys
                                          pink the girls
                                          ugly, pretty,
                                          white or black
                                          attached to you -
                      nor the pressures of fast or slow
                      Because that's not your mandate

                      Your mandate is simply to grow

In the fullness of time,
there is time enough
for you to be the best that you can be
But for now, you ought to live in life's simplicity

Because there is a sense of ought-ness in you
I see it shining through

IT'S A BOY!

It's a boy!
It's a girl!
It's a fine baby
Black and beautiful
From head to toe
But they only reason
You don't think so
Is because 300 years ago
You literally lost your mind

MISLED

Riding on an uptown subway train
On our way to seeing a Christmas show
My three year old said to me
"Daddy, can we sing a song?"

I said, "Okay baby"
Then started singing

"Yes, Jesus loves me
Yes, Jesus loves me
Yes, Jesus loves me
For the Bible tells me so"

She said, "No, Daddy, not that song
Let's sing a *Christ*-mas song"

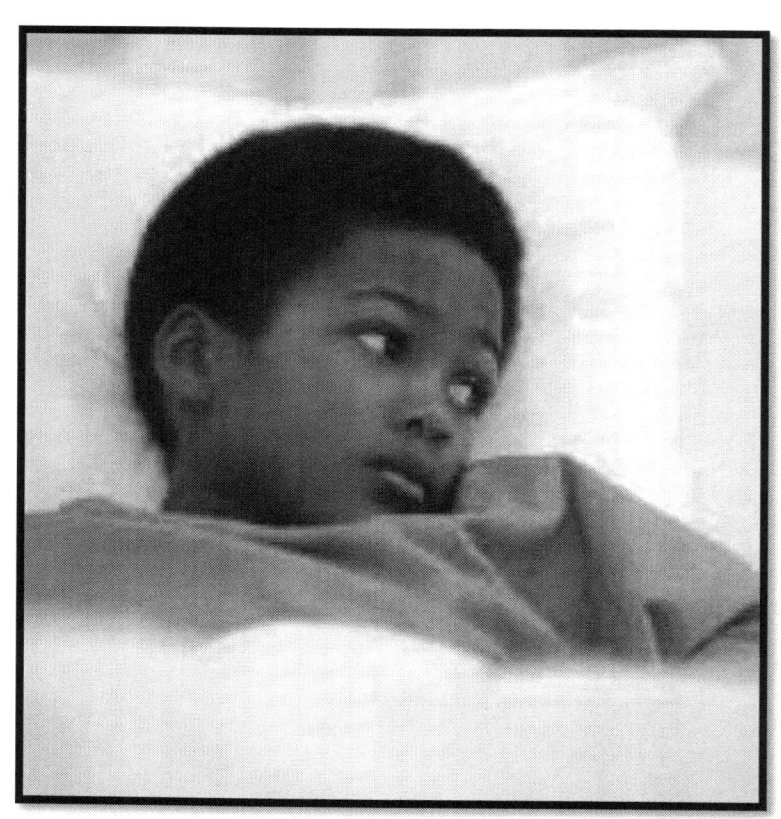

TERRENCE FAGAN SMILED TODAY

Beaten, like hail falling
On a tin garbage can
Torn apart at the seams

Scorned, with scars
never to be replaced
Feeling withdrawn
And a bit out of place

Emotions bottled up
with the precision of seltzer water
Painful reminders that the
hurt was still there

Slowly, he emerged from his coma
Relieved to see his mother
though she was dripping with tears

It had been 6 long weeks
since the last of these "incidents"
But it was finally done
She had waited too long
and heard too many "I'm sorry 's"
She had to admit
that he couldn't love her
and wouldn't love Terrence, her son

This time, it was nearly fatal
Perhaps, a heartbeat away
But she knew now that
everything would be all right
Because Terrence Fagan smiled today

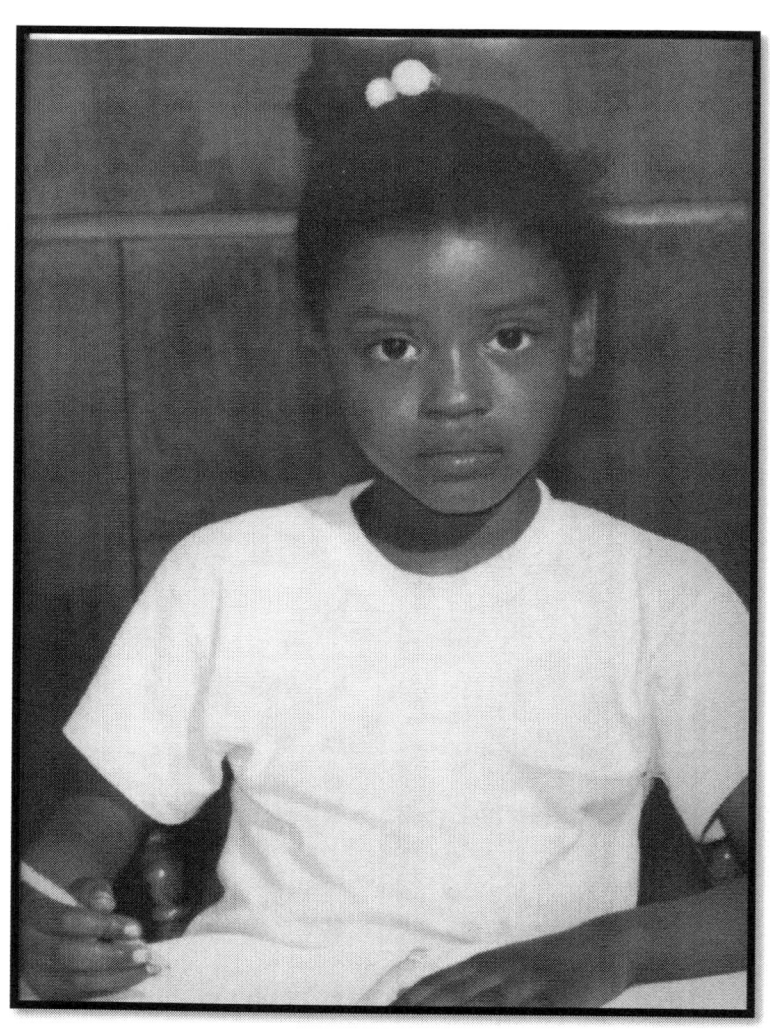

EXPECTATIONS

Where there's no great expectation
there can be no great disappointment

A little black child living in the ghetto ruins of one of our urban promise lands was sitting in her third-grade classroom one day when she was approached by her teacher. "Tomorrow," said the teacher, "I want you and the rest of the class to bring a used plastic dinner plate to school."

And so the next day arrived and the teacher stood before the children and said, "Today we're going to use these dinner plates that you've brought to school on a class project. We are going to write something on the plates called a - 20 year will." Immediately, one of her students raised his hand and asked,

"What's a will?"

"A will," said the teacher "is a document that projects things into the future. It's a piece of writing, which outlines how you would like your future to unfold.
I want you to write on your plate, in your own words, all of your desires, wishes, wants, needs and aspirations. I want you to write down on the plates how you see yourself.

"Not how you see yourself now" said the teacher, "but how and where you see yourself 20 years from now. Some of you are going to be doctors and lawyers; some will be astronauts, technicians and teachers while others may become bankers or bricklayers. Whatever you wish to be, whatever you want to be, that is what I want you to write on your plate.

After you write your 20-year will on the plates, we will paint over what you have written with an invisible paint.

And when it dries, you may take your plate home to show your families. But save the plates! Said the teacher, "because who knows! In 20 years, you may want to look back on your plate and see how close you came to achieving your goals."

"The only thing that I would caution you about" said the teacher, "this should be an individual exercise. Please try not to copy your classmate's writing but use your own words."

The little black girl thought about it for a few minutes, then she picked up a pen and began to write.
This is what she wrote:

> *To my absent father, my alcoholic mother and her mean boyfriend*
> *To my grandmamma, - who I know don't really want me to come stay with her Down South next summer*
> *To the landlord - who won't ever fix that broken elevator or send us no heat in the wintertime*
> *To my best friend - who I saw smoking dope in the hallway but never told anybody*
> *To the crack addicts - who broke into the mailbox and stole my momma's check for the fourth time this year*

She said:

> *This is for the lady who lives next door - who said I was R-E-A-L black and ugly*
> *To the man in the candy store who tried to feel my behind*
> *And to the teacher - who I overheard joking with another teacher that all these ghetto kids are so stupid and so dumb*

With tears rolling down her face, the little girl concluded her writings by saying –

20 years from now, I'll try NOT to live up to your expectations of me.

I PLEDGE ALLEGIANCE

I pledge allegiance
to the idea
that I am an unrepeatable
gift to this universe

That life is pregnant with possibilities
and though the odds may seem high -
I am highly favored

I am in agreement
that what I do today
will decide my fate tomorrow,
That success won't come to me - I must go to it

In my pursuit of excellence
I will have no failure - only feedback
            no enemies - just teachers
            no problems - just challenges
                      which I will rise to meet

I pledge allegiance
that my reach
will exceed my grasp
But if I fall - I will get up

For there is no shame in not reaching my goals
but in not having any goals to reach

I pledge allegiance
that the sum total of my parts
does not equal my whole
That in Christ
I am more than a conqueror
And no one
can make me feel inferior
without my consent

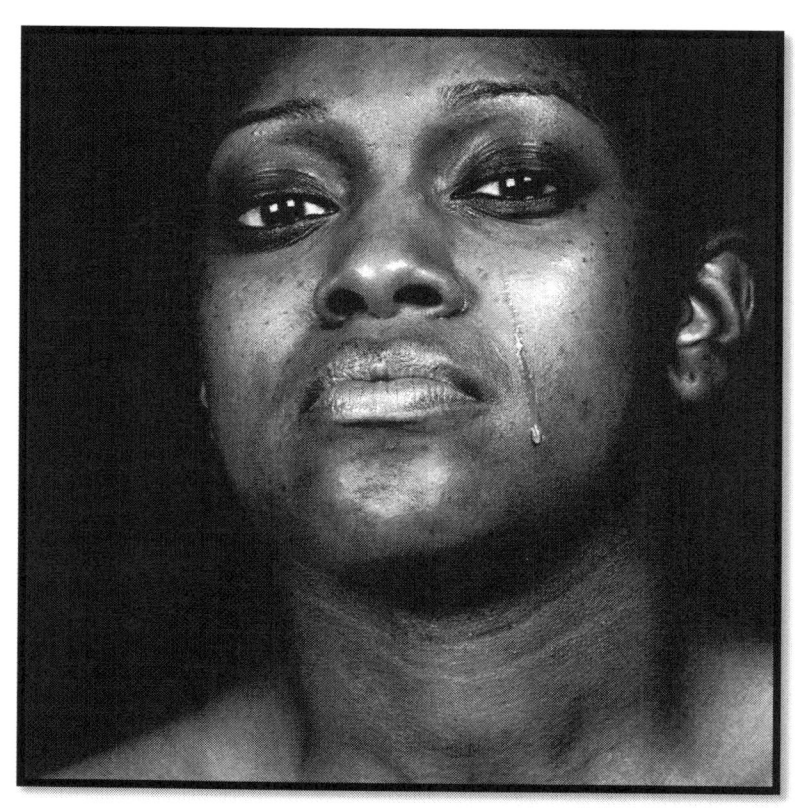

THE 23ᴿᴰ PSALM

by Layding Kaliba

She sat there reading the 23rd Psalm
She read it over and over trembling
cold sweat pouring from her body
tears rolling from puffed eyes
skin
        pale and lifeless

Outside her window
she could still hear
chatter and screams of
wildlife that roamed
her South Bronx
        jungle habitat

She knew that somewhere
hidden beneath the blanket of
New York City's bestiality
the monkey,
the real king of the jungle
        laid in wait

For 17 years the monkey
had ridden her back growing fat
off life sucked from her veins
for 17 years she tried unsuccessfully
to dethrone the king
to purge herself of the jungle fever
that had placed her on the brink of death
but on this night the monkey would
claim no victim
she dug deep into the pocket of her
        will to survive
found God and together they
ripped the monkey from her back
        "The Lord is my shepherd"

Over and over into the night she read
holding desperately to this new found
lease on life

she had to live, she had to live
she kept telling herself
not just for herself
but for her eight-year-old daughter
who had grown-up in her mother's battle
                                      grounds
choking from the dust of the battle
wading in the cesspool of the
                              South Bronx jungle

She wondered if her daughters eyes
could penetrate the storms
                              of her existence

could she stepped outside the confusion
                              and fear
learn the lessons of her mother's nightmare
life had so vividly told her

Had her eyes zoomed in for close-ups
of the battle scenes ,the swollen eyes
puffed hands and track scarred arms

Had she witnessed vultures that hovered
over her mother's misfortune
jackals waiting to feast on the remains
of a lost struggle. Leeches that sucked
the life blood of her dreams

Over and over she read
praying between verses
hoping her daughter understood
that the fever had been broken
the battle had been won
and that the 23rd Psalms
was a celebration
of victory speech
a new beginning
                "The Lord is my shepherd"
                "The Lord Is my shepherd"

ERASE

Said a grade school teacher
to a third-grade schoolboy -
"If you make a mistake on your paper,
you may use your eraser
to erase your mistake"

And the little boy corrected his
errors by simply erasing them

Said two parents one day to their
11-year-old Sixth-grade son:
"We made a mistake by getting married
It's just not working out
So we're getting a divorce
But we love you very, very much"

And they dissolve their problem
by simply obtaining a divorce

Said a 20-year-old second-year college
Student after learning his girlfriend was
two months pregnant:
"Listen, I think we made a mistake
I'm not ready for all of this —
Get rid of it"

ADULTHOOD

I wish adulthood had a formula
for taking care of babies and fools
The way it was when I was a child

Wish it had a forget-me-not
insurance policy
so I could forget the pain
that growing up tends to follow

You see, it's been my experience that
adulthood doesn't take too kindly to
                              torn sleeves
                              smelly socks or
                              dirty blue jeans

I find it to be far less tolerant of
runny noses
incomplete homework and
"oops - I forgot to brush my teeth ma"

When you're a child,
it's all right if you trip and fall —
in fact, it's kinda cute
                But falling down in adulthood
                seldom yields much laughter

                        15-year-olds
                        standing on street corners
                        in high heels, offering cheap thrills
                        to men four times their age
                        makes me wonder —
                        What is it in life they're really after?

Funny thing about life -
It offers little protection to those who can't make the
connection from foolishness to maturation.

Life will drop kick and body slam you in an effort to
break your spirit - but don't take it personally

All of us will get a glimpse of our destiny
but few-there-be, who will come near it

Because growing up dictates that life is
ridden without its training wheels

It's a rite of passage that's painfully real -
Real is the misery
and the suffering supplied
It's the coming of womanhood
but the dignity denied

It's the inevitable struggle
to make ends meet
It's "*child! My rent is paid up
but we ain't got a thing to eat*"

It's projects, rejects,
and broken elevator doors
Dreams stored in bottles of
bargain-basement self -esteem
but top shelf pity

It's called life
Flip it over and
it ain't so pretty

How much pain must we endure
under the illusion that we're mature?

Wouldn't it be nice if we could return to a
time when life was simple and pristinely gay
When fun was had in an effortless way

It seems to me, if we are to progress
then maybe we should regress-
instead of always meddling
We should ride through life
the way a 3 year-old rides her bike
but notice how she never falls off -
unless she stops pedaling

AND MADE IT LOOK NATURAL

I created you
           and made it look natural
Nurtured you
           until you were grown
I stretched
           and you had skies
Coughed
           and there was wind
Blinked
           and your sun was on
Split
           and you had friend
I did all this for you
           and made it look natural
But then you forgot about me
Now you're trying to artificially grow
           as if you ever could
Why in the world would you do that
           I just don't know
           and believe me - I should

SANCTIMONIOUS SAUCE

Sandwiched somewhere between
Your religious bread rolls
Magnanimous mayonnaise
Orthodox onions
Legitimized lettuce
Tempestuous tomatoes
Dogmatic dressing
Pious pepper
And Sanctimonious salt

I find it difficult to taste your faith

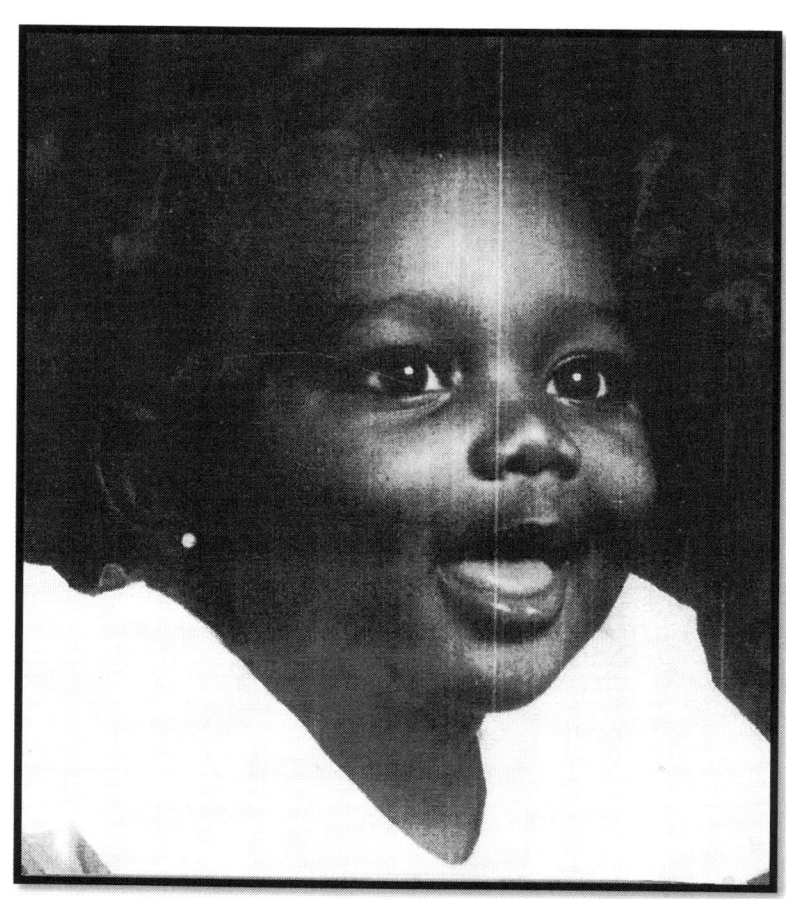

WINNER

(There is none more beautiful)

My bright and sunny brown baby girl
On your face - there's a look that shows
A smile that glows - so beautiful

Under the conditions of which you were born
It becomes all the more clear -
YOU ARE A WINNER BABY!
And we're so glad you made it here

Your birth makes it all worthwhile
The soothing sound of your cry
Is a welcome change
To your mother and I
From the thunder rolls of life

The breath you breathe
Has somehow relieved
The weariness of our strife
The life you live
Gives joy to a pair of souls
Filled with sorrow
Each day you grow -we know
There's a better tomorrow

BECAUSE YOU ARE A WINNER BABY!

And with that comes a spirit
That owns the sky
It explores and conquers
With hope that never dies

You will carry the load and
Pave the road to success
Hold your head up high
And walk with pride
For unto you belongs the best

My bright and sunny brown baby flower
The tears you now cry
Your mother and I
Can easily wipe away

But you must understand
There will come a day
When living won't seem so fair

Remember to keep the faith
Because with faith -
You can master all things
Try to remain calm about
The storm, which rages
Over your youthful head

Be aware there's a SOURCE
That you can rely on
Understand - God is not dead

You were born black and feminine
In a "glass-ceiling" world
Daring you to submit or perish

But you survived
And it is your life
we now cherish

You come from a long line of
Survivors because all Blacks are
Fighters from the womb to the tomb
Even though it's been
An uphill battle
We've managed to succeed

I now give you this advice
And it is the only weapon
That you will ever need

"MY BRIGHT AND SUNNY
BROWN BABY GIRL
YOU ARE A WINNER!
AND THIS IS YOUR WORLD"

WOMEN

Women are strong - cause they gotta be.
Especially the woman who carried me

Women must be strong to right the
wrongs that's been around for years
Like the wrong that says men can abuse
them and all they'll get back is tears

Women must be strong for
reasons, which I already knew
Stronger than the myth that between
the sexes - they're the weaker of the two

Women helped build dynasties while
conducting an Underground Railroad
Picked cotton, cooked food, cleaned clothes
plus carried the load of being a mother

They sit on the Board, run the business
and they're always ready to create
They do 9 to 5's while being our wives
but still find time to educate

Women pay rent and put food
on the table when we're not able
Heal our babies by holding them tight -
lead the struggle for equal rights

Think about the woman who wiped
your snotty nose and dried your
crying eyes when you found out
you weren't so much of a man after all
Fed you when you are hungry, sheltered
you and never let your spirits fall

Yeah. Women are strong!

But besides all that — they're beautiful
just to look at. Don't you agree?

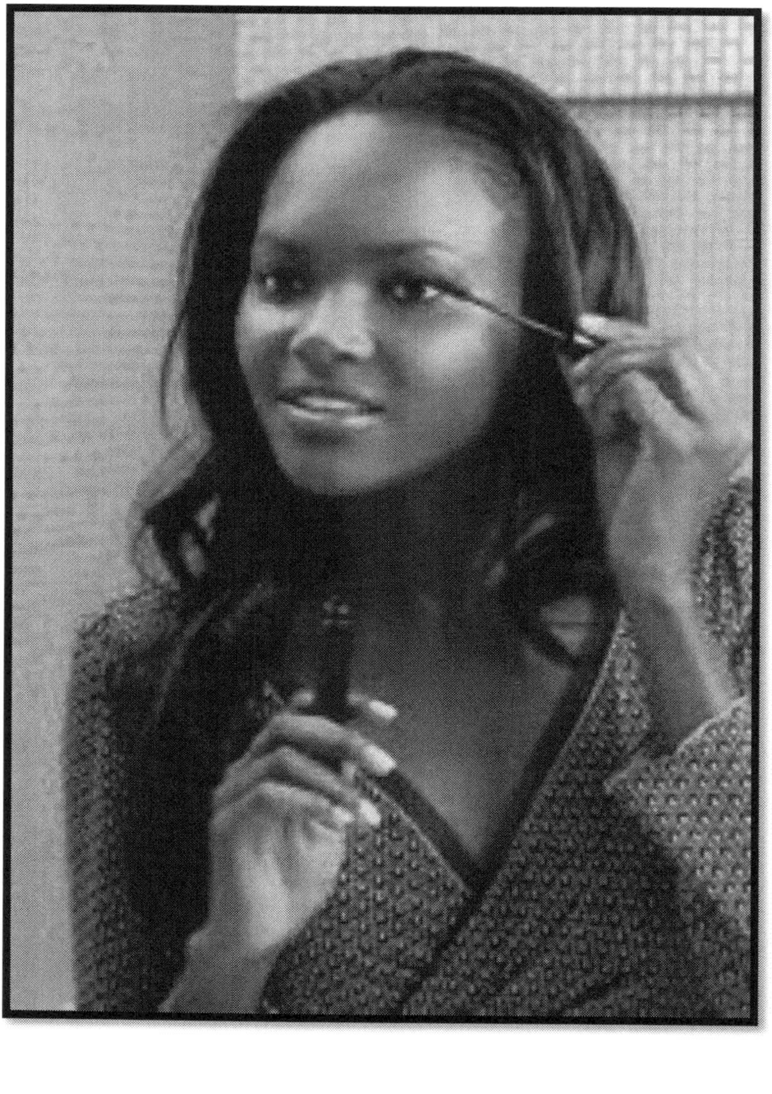

IF A GIRL ISN'T PRETTY

If a girl isn't pretty
where it really matters most -
In the deepest part of her being

Regardless of what the world is seeing
She has nothing she can boast

If a girl isn't pretty
beyond her face and hair -
In the deepest part of her joy

Despite what her mirror swears
She is not pretty, but void

If her whole world is
based on being gorgeous
and nothing more in return

If it's twisted on lies
and bent on beauty
If sex appeal
is what she yearns

If she muses her skin
but neglects to see
the beauty within
She hasn't seen herself

For if a girl isn't pretty
where it really counts -
In the deepest part of her soul,
her imprisoned splendor
simply cannot surrender
the real beauty, she's yet to behold

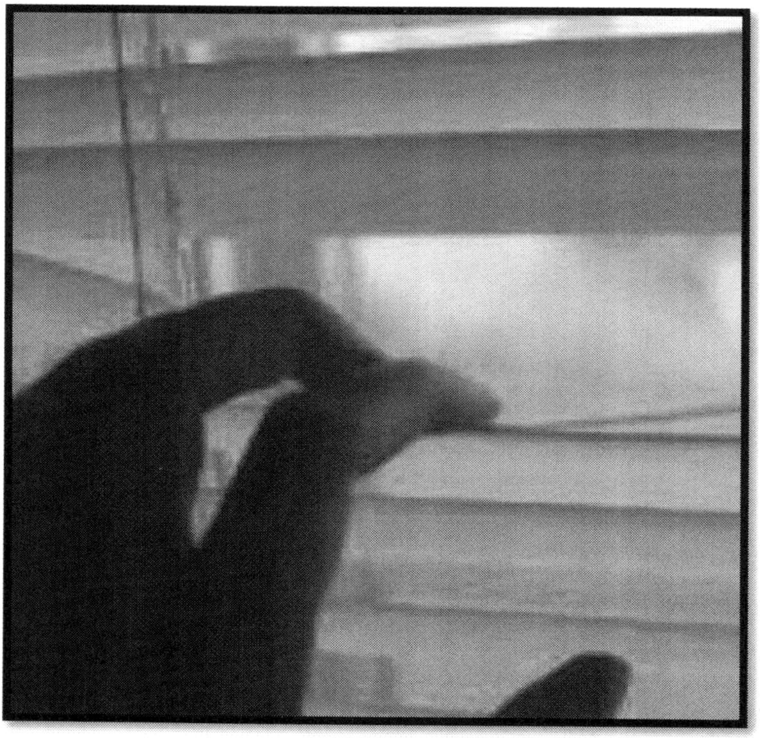

HOW MANY LIES

How many lies can you tell
When your lover has left
When your woman, your wife,
the mother of your child - is gone?

How many ways can you convince
yourself that you must be strong -
cause crying just ain't allowed?

How much better could you feel
about the fact that -
it ain't your fault?
What does it mean to be proud?

How many times can you tell
your neighbors that they just
missed her? That "she took the kids
to the in-laws and won't be back
'til late tonight?"

How long can you insist that she
was wrong and you were right?

How long can you stare at old
photographs and make up excuses
when you know - she just ain't there?

How many times did you peek out the
window, or wait for the mailman
How many ways did you swear?

How many lies can you tell
is the name of the game
What is it about the truth
that causes us so much pain?

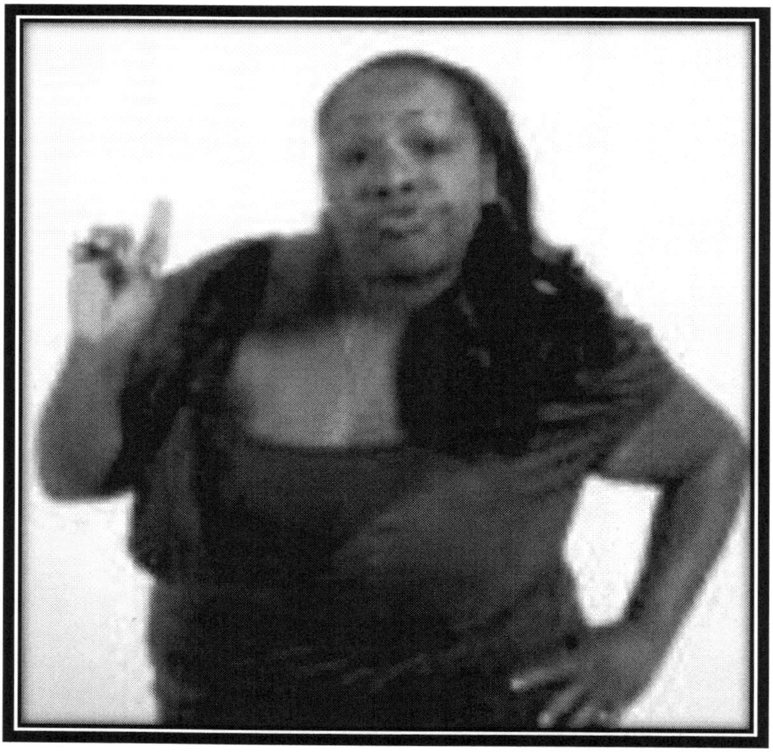

SUNDAY TO BE EXACT

I was walkin' down the street the other day.
It was Sunday to be exact
Cause I'd just come from buyin'
three pieces of greasy fried chicken - and a biscuit

That's when I heard some singin' comin' from
this little ole storefront church across the street
and C-H-I-L-D! - It was soundin' good!
So good, I had to cross over
so I could hear it better

They were singin' a song called "Nobody Loves Anybody
All the Time Except My Sweet Jesus!"
And they were gittin' all undignified
It was one of them holy-rolly sanctified halleluiah churches.
H-O-N-E-Y, the saints were just-a hand-clappin' and a foot-stompin' until it made you wanna *MOOVE* yourself!

I sat my big be-hind on top of the hood of a parked car
in front of the church, opened up my box of chicken
and started greasin' right there

Honey, God knows they were singin' that song for me

They got louder and louder and kept on singin' - "NOBODY LOVES ANYBODY ALL THE TIME EXCEPT MY SWEET JESUS!"

Well, I finished my chicken and stayed there
'til my eyes had done dried
Then, I cleaned up my mess and went on home

I figured they were singin' that song for me
cause they knew I was gonna be walkin' by
They knew that my man had done left me
and they wanted me to know why
Oh, he said it was cause I was about 100 pounds too fat,
and he was tired of pretendin' by calling it "pleasingly-plump." Guess I didn't please him know mo'
But the real reason my man left me was because —
NOBODY LOVES ANYBODY ALL THE TIME EXCEPT. . . . .

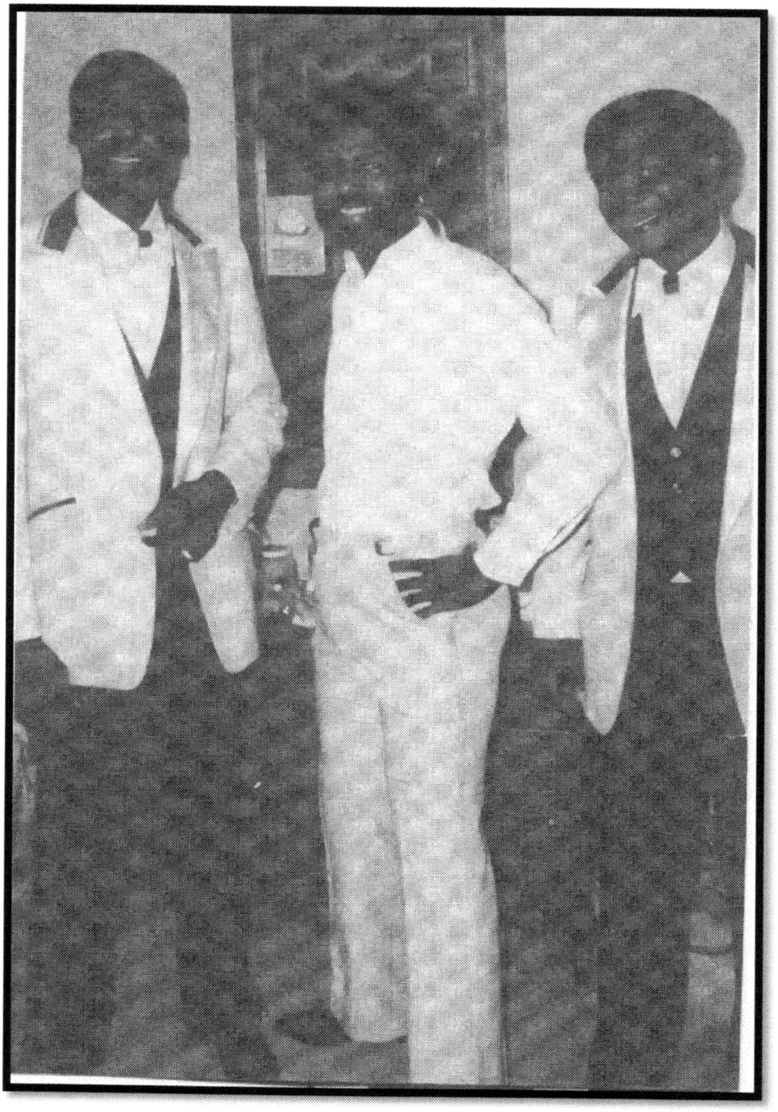

A FEW GOOD MEN

Brothers, if the NBA, NFL and the major leagues have turned you down, then why don't you join my team

I'm looking for a few good men

Men who are mindful of what manhood is about

Who know the task and can get the job done

I'm seeking men that respect their wives
                their women
                their race
    but most of all — themselves

Calling all men who don't want to be or even need to be
                superfly
                superbad or
                superfresh - just super
                          fathers

I need men who can raise their families —
instead of their fists
Who get a real big kick out of watching their
children grow, rather than kicking their women

I'm looking for a few good men

Please be on the lookout for sensitive men
with a higher agenda
Brothers who thought about giving it up,
but refused to surrender
Men who are holistically inclined through their
                            spirit and soul
Who are ambitious by nature but clear with their goals

I need men who are cognizant that manhood is more about
dignity and perseverance than sexual dominance
Men who can stretch their minds-instead of their penises
Who can build up nations - rather than just "bust-a-nut"
Who can spread knowledge and wisdom —
as opposed to their filthy lust
I say - I'm looking for a few good men

Give me a man who ain't got nothin' to prove
Men that refuse to prostitute their ethics
                deny their sex
                or lose their racial identity

I need men to grow up, and leave their boyhood
games behind
to stop bouncing balls,
      smoking dope or
           standing on street corners - drinking wine

Listen, my brother!

If you wear your manhood
high on your chest with honor-
if it suits you just fine
If you're so comfortable with it
that it radiates and shines
Then I want you to get together with me —
and together we'll try
We're gonna destroy the myth
We're gonna tear down the lie

That a good man is hard to find!

FINDERS -KEEPERS

I found the condoms you hid
Shall I tell you where?
You lost another chance to love me last night
Do you really care?

This is the third time this year you misplaced
your wedding ring - but who's counting?
I found two more phone numbers in your
shirt pockets - just business I presume
No mis-phone calls today
but the hang-ups are mounting

Too bad, you don't take care your business
Like you take care your lovin'
Shame, you don't handle your responsibilities
The way you handle your lies

You Lose, I Find - We Hurtin'

SOMETHING IN THE MIRROR FRIGHTENED ME

    Jealous eyes
    Cut throat
    Lying tongue
    Tattered hair - gray and worn

    Stale grin
    Pale skin
    Long face
    Envy green, scarlet scorn

    Nose poked
    Ears bent
    Back stabbed
    Body aching with pain

    Head bowed
    Knees buckled
    Mind blown
    Since you left, nothing's the same

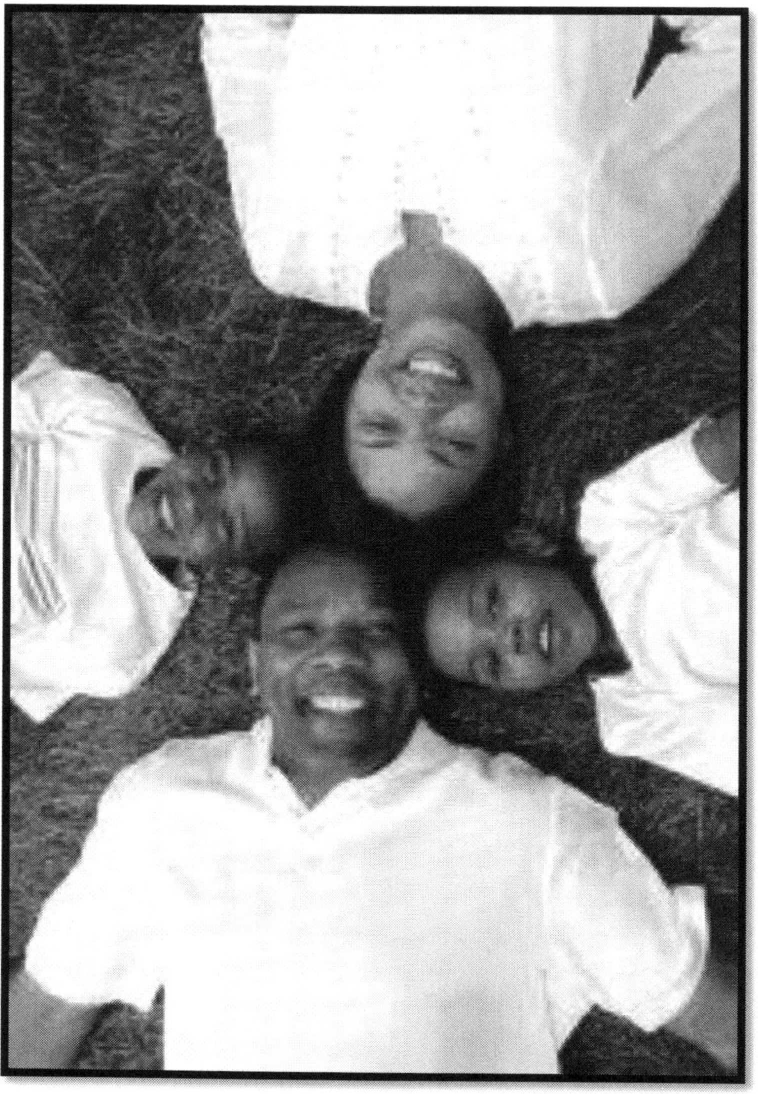

FREE TO BE A FAMILY

And when you're able to quarterback your family as well as you quarterback your favorite team - showing strength, agility and Herculean ability to go the distance

When you can look at a woman and
resist the temptation for sex
but see her as a complete human being
whom God has chosen to complement man

When you feel again what you
felt for her in the beginning
And remember how good it was

When the only thing in the doghouse is the dog

When you're most adoring fans-
your children and wife
are cheering you on
because you're sober tonight

When you discover the nuances
between caretaking and caregiving
and stop living as if you have 1000 years

When you can reach for the sky
but keep your feet on the ground
And lift yourself up
without tearing others down
       — YOU ARE

When you believe in yourself
even as others doubt you
yet rise above their rain -
Replacing the pain of their finger-pointing
with the universal gesture of a smile

When you discover that you cannot
control the actions of others
but you can master your reactions

When you stop majoring in minor things

and understand that the earth
is the lord's and the fullness thereof

When helping your children navigate
the emotional, social and politically
polluted waters of life is more important
than a divorce
                         - YOU ARE FREE

When you can feed both your
family and your inspiration
no longer sleeping with anger,
or rising with rage

When you can raise your family
instead of your fist
and learn that
love is never abusive

When you realize that she is
not immune to softness
and recognize that you
will not be elevated
until womankind is liberated

Finally,
when you can build your home
before building your house,
then you are truly. . . . . . . FREE
. . . . TO BE
. . . . A FAMILY

TAKE THESE BROKEN WINGS

Freshly loose shackles
Overworked mules
Underpaid hands
And nowhere to land

Take these broken wings

Empty pockets
Bare cupboards
Crusty stale bread
And young-uns to be fed

Take these broken wings

Sin in disguise
Homelessness on the rise
Preachers on the take
And families about the break

Babies having babies
Schools ain't schooling
And the streets ain't fooling

Assassinated leaders
Drugs that defeat us
And police that beat us

Take these broken wings - and learn to fly

ANYBODY CAN

Anybody can like you when you're riding high
Anybody can enjoy you, anybody can lie
But always remember
The world can change again
You might have to go slow
You may have to bend
When your pockets are low
See how many friends you got
When you ain't got

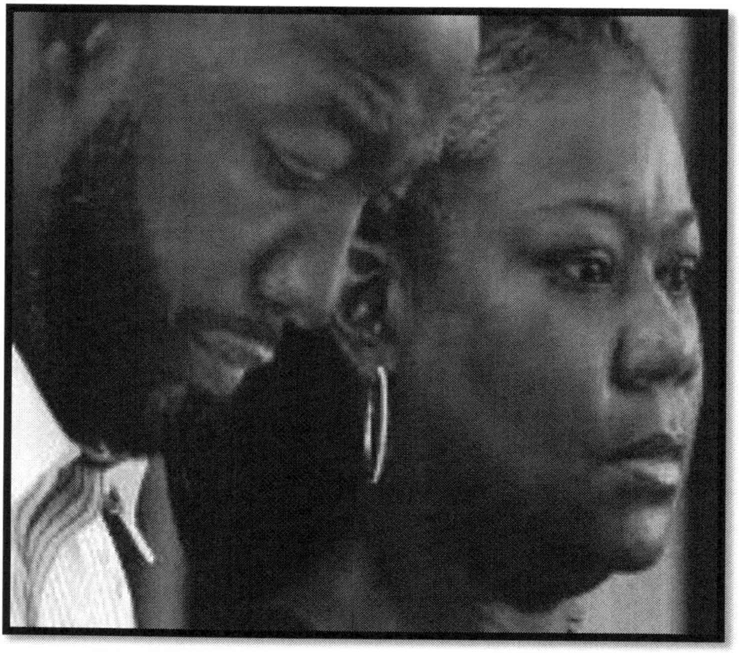

METAPHOR OF LIFE

There is much sadness in the metaphor of life
But there is even more sorrow

I promise you no end to the tears

I will not forget you
though at times, I shall try

I will deny your death in the metaphor
Then in the real sense, I will laugh
because you left me behind

The patterns that were cut so deeply
shall forever be yours
but I warn you - the fabric will be mine

I will manufacture smiles
enough to disguise
my emptiness and void

The meters of the distance
        the rate
        and the time since you've been gone,
        will be measured

But in the metaphor of life,
The fact that I once held you
so tightly in my arms - can only be treasured

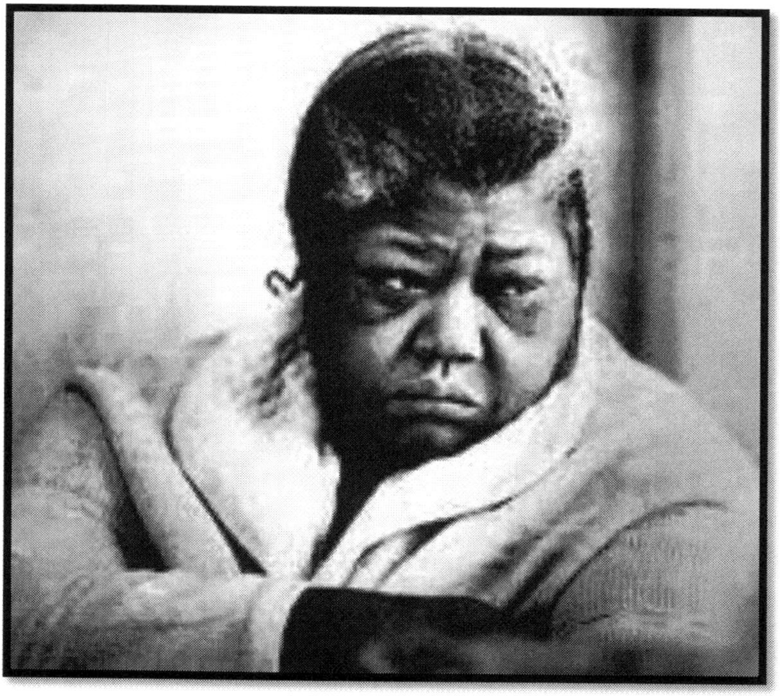

OPEN DOOR POLICY

When they knocked on her door, I wonder if she was reading a high school history book. If so, I wonder how far did she get in her reading.

I suspect she had completed the section on Africa, Australia, Europe, and the Americas and was in the midst of reading about Asia when she discovered a pattern.

Somewhere in the text, it must have said that the world is a global community; a place where people and nations are interdependent upon one another for their common survival; where food, geography, climate, culture and ideas must be shared and respected. All good textbooks on history say this kind of stuff.

But suddenly, when she reached the section on Asia, and looked at the pictures, it must've dawned on her. These were all people of color - perhaps distant relatives of hers. They were all forcibly uprooted, degraded, and exploited by the Europeans under the guise of "we are a global community."

While they were yet knocking on her door, I suspect she was actually reading how the Chinese government "distrusted" the Westerners and how they refused to allow them into their country.

Perhaps she knew why and adopted this as her personal policy. That is when, in 1984, a more local group of Westerners adopted their own policy and named it "open door policy."

That is when Eleanor Bumpers, a 300 pound 66 year old arthritic grandmother, had her apartment door kicked opened by the New York City Finest and received two bullets in her chest as an eviction notice.

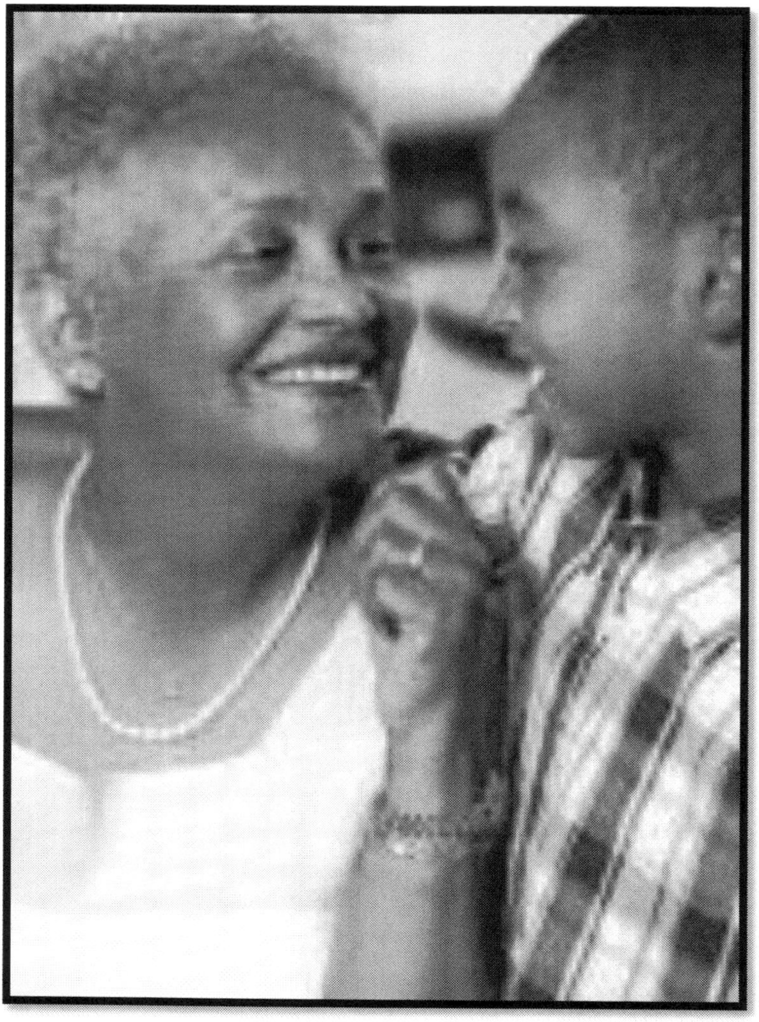

SWEET POTATO PIE

You used to grease my face
on cold and bitter winter days
And I heard you when you said —
>"*Get up off that floor boy!*
>*Lying down for us just ain't*
>*gonna ever be the way*
>*We the kind of people*
>*who ne-e-eds to keep pushin' on*
>*God knows! We done been lied*
>*about. We been in the storm*"

Every Sunday morning
I'd hear you say -
>"*Hurry up Child! You better get*
>*out that bed. We got to make the*
>*service on time. God ain't crazy*
>*'bout no lazy che'ren. I tell you,*
>*He just don't care for them kind*"

Although I don't make
the services much like
I use to   -   Sweet Potato Pie
              I miss you
              Sweet Potato Pie
              I miss you

You taught me to say: "Our Father, which art in
              Heaven, Hallowed be thy name"
              But you were the only father
              or mother that I ever knew

You were my bright and shining sun
My Gr-e-a-t gettin' up mornin'!
My kingdom Come

You use to bake hot buttered biscuits
and sweet potato pies
as often as I could remember
Each time, it came
with a great big smile
You could make me
feel real good about myself

even when I didn't intend to

But   -   Sweet Potato Pie
        I been missing you
        Sweet Potato Pie
        I miss you

You said to me - "*Boy, sometimes you do gets to be a little tired. And you feels the need for a cool drink of water. But don't you sit at that well too long, boy!*
Nah, 'cause there's work to be done

The world ain't got no shortage of people who wants to beat you down. They tries to break your spirit but don't you let nobody put you under Stand up and be a man!
Never shy away from your responsibilities Do the best you can

Give it your all boy
Til you can't do no more
And if you ever need a little help-
That's what I'm here for"

Oh! But now you're gone grandma

And I say   -   Sweet Potato Pie
            I been missing you
            Sweet Potato Pie
            I sure been missing you!

TELL ME TOMORROW

As sure as there is bad news in this world,
There are those who surely love to deliver it.

Oh Trouble – Beware!
You are not welcome here

I am not suited for you
And I do not wear you well

But what is bothering thy bearer's soul
He has swallowed it whole
And with dripping lips
is so eager to tell

For his door is wide open
And there -
You may surely stay
But when you're knocking at my door
I hear not thy lure
And in time,
You will indeed go away

So if it is sour news
You're seeking to lose
Oh great bearer of much sorrow
If trouble has the haunted
with its horror and fright
You must tell me of it tomorrow,
cause I'm just not gonna let you
bother me tonight!

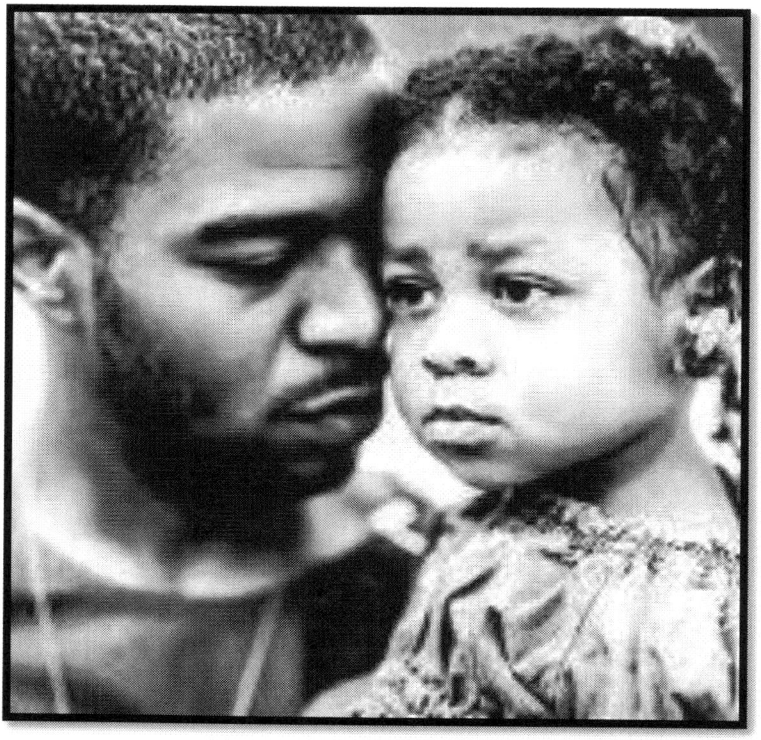

SORRY ABOUT THE CONFUSION

Dear daughter,

At two years old, you could not possibly understand what's going on around you, though you can identify with the hurt. Waking you up in the middle of a purposeful sleep after you've had a busy day, jumping, climbing, sliding and running just for the joy of it - is purposeless. I will accept full responsibility for it because I've already accepted the shame.

Making your two year old brain ponder the meaning of having two homes, two beds, two churches, two Christmases, two Easters, two birthday parties, two Thanksgivings Dinners and having to share two different hearts that love you is, I know - a bit too much to bear. I think even Noah would agree.

Hearing you repetitively ask the inevitable question, "Why Daddy, why can't I stay here a little longer?" is heartbreaking. Although I possess a Master's degree, I have not yet mastered how to give you an intelligent answer. You see it was never intended that you should suffer from the residual effects of our dilemma.

Please believe me when I say that it is not your fault. Yet I don't think I exaggerate when I say it is actually no one's fault. There is no good guy and there is no bad guy. There is only your mother and I - and we simply disagree.

Hearing you tell me over the phone "I love you daddy" is of course the next best thing to having you tell me with a kiss and a great big hug. With you not knowing Monday from Sunday, it's deeply painful when you ask me to pick you up and I have to respond — "next weekend baby."

Dear daughter,

How can I tell someone as bright as you that your mother and I are arguing over a pair of socks accidentally left over here, a child support check that was late arriving there, an earring lost and a time boarder crossed - is there no end to this madness?

How do I explain that in some cases you are fortunate to have two caring parents in an era where most of your peers do not? Is there some consolation in the fact that I will be there for you on your first day of school? And I will be at your first school play and I will rise on Easter morning to hear you say "He rose." There will be two hands pushing you on your next bicycle ride. I think you know that I love you and your mother does too. And yes, this *is* a funny way of showing it.

Dear daughter,

One day you'll understand what's happening here - maybe one day you won't have to. I knew that in your growing up, there would be much pain. I knew life would eventually become more complicated and many things would be out of its normal order, but I never dreamed that so soon, at your tender age, you would have to concern yourself with wondering what happened to your beautiful world.

Dear daughter,

I'm sorry about the confusion.

FAMILY PORTRAIT

One day, for some reason
a long, long time ago
a group of people came together
to take a picture they
would all be very proud to show

Now, these were no ordinary people —
Oh! No! Not indeed
They were all very close to me.
You might say, of the same seed

And many years later,
as I look back at this picture,
there is joy in my heart
For in this very picture,
my most loving memories start

In this same picture,
I can see good times and bad
with troubles a few
High times and low times
Yet we all came through

As I look deeper into it
I'm sensing more details
More sights, more colors
more sounds and yes -more smells

There's my uncles Willie and Mike
They always did so much for me
They took me to all those places
So just like my friends, I too could see

There's Aunt Betty and Uncle Carl
Who moved out of the city
After all these years they're still together
And my goodness! Don't they look pretty?

As I gaze into the portrait
There's Karen and there's Tricia
with Kevin and Junior
First cousin, second cousin
And even some who may fool ya

I see girlfriends and boyfriends
and children so sweet
Without them in this picture
it would not be complete

Hey! There's Penny, my sister
and Stevie, my little brother
"Always take care of him,"
Mama used to say
"Cause you don't have another"

Yeah!

It's good to see mama smile
and even laugh sometimes
She worked so hard to give us the best
So hard so we could be like the rest

I'll never forget how they all sacrificed
and always love them for what they shared
Looking back on this picture
I'm so proud of them today
and even happier they cared

But there's one person missing
from all of the rest

One person that's not in this picture
Who I never knew

One person that even they
could not suppress

AIN'T IN THE MOOD

Ain't in the mood for blu-u-ues tonight!
Tonight Evvvvrrrything gotta be alright- you know why? My baby's comin' home and
She done been gone for too long
So I says, my fault honey -
I was wrong

Then, I commenced to cleanin' up de place until it was just spic and span
You know, I *finally* washed dem old dirty dishes
I mops de flo'
I even put out de garbage can!

Well, she got homeabout a quarter past ten

Took one look at me
and broke on out in a gr-r-r-reat big grin
I said -
"Good God, woman! I MISS YOU SO!
Can't stands it, iff'n you'd ever le-e-e-eaves me again
'Cause I just ain't in the mo-o-o-ood for blu-u-u-ues tonight!

You know - we talked a little while
Then we hit that ole sack
I started whispering sweet nothings in her ear
And she whispered right on back

Oooooo, we rocked and we rolled
'Til the ear-r-r-rly mornin' dawn
Next thing I went to turn over and
Don't you know! That woman was gone

So, I jumps up quickly
Started searchin' all through de house
Only thing that I could find
was a note she left
in de cabinet of the bathroom
It said, "You no good SOB!
This here bottle wasn't my perfume"

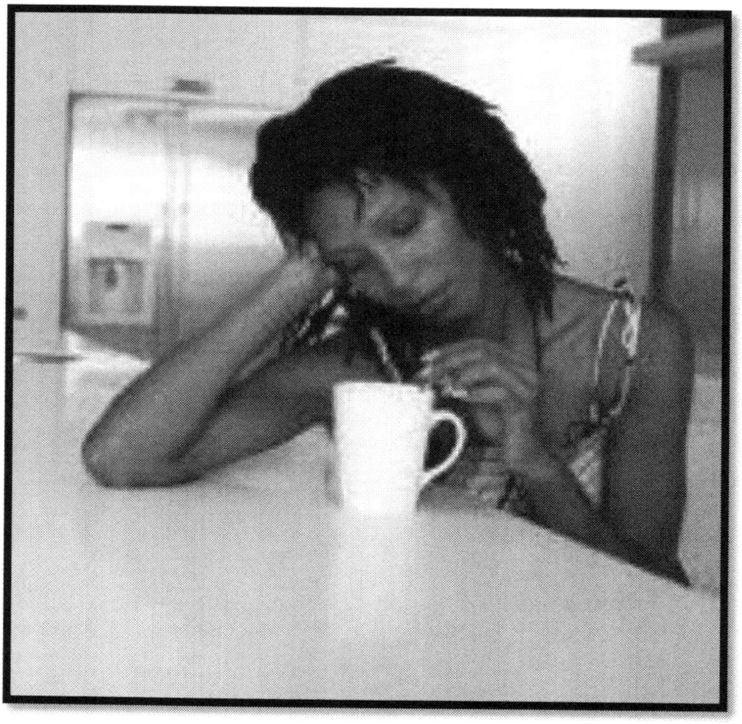

CAN'T SMILE IT AWAY

It's been one year
One year since you've been gone

One year since I've seen you,
                caressed you,
                argued with you -
                        laughed with you

The sun is still its brightest in the summer
Flowers still bloom in the spring and
leaves continually descend in the fall

Still, it's been one year and I
want your presence - but need your warmth
want your touch - but need your sensitivity
want your company - but need your love
I need to hear from you

It's been one whole year

The soap dish is always messy
The faucet drips
and I still forget to put the toilet seat up
and the window shades down
I enjoy soft music
with dimly lit bedroom lights
I haven't stopped burning the dinner rolls
but my coffee is just right

I still cry from watching late night movies
and laugh at your ridiculous baby pictures

But it's been one year since you've been gone
And when I think about that —
I just can't smile it away

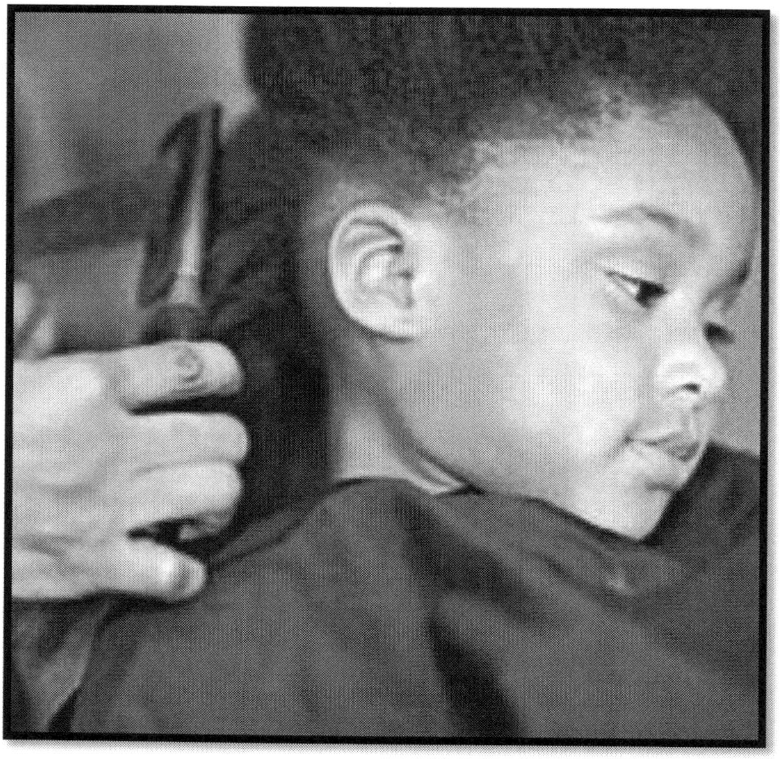

NYEMA (Ny-ee-mah)

Nyema didn't know about
Red Clay, Blue-Black Funk or
the prodigious Georgia Heat

Living in a polyester world,
She'd never heard of Hot Cotton fields,
Windy City blues, Ground floor-rear door
back of the bus – SOUL

Nothing she would ever do
could prepare her for the Greyhound
               Cornbread
                    Kentucky Fried Blues
                             of an era gone by

She wasn't
hip to a Bessie, a Billie,
or a 'Lonely Teardrop' called Jackie

She didn't know there was such a thing
called "Jumping with the Count"
"Swinging with the Duke" or
Singing with the Divine Miss Sarah Vaughn
or any other blue-blooded black skinned legend

Though Nyema was sassy!

She had yet to be introduced to
                        a Horn named Lena,
                        a Bird called Charlie
                        or a Train named Cole

With each passing day it became increasingly harder
to describe this thing called – SOUL

What she doesn't understand is -
the Aretha she now hears,
to be Judgment-Day-Honest, ain't quite as good as
she used to be, but she still gets 'R-E-S-P-E-C-T'

She doesn't quite comprehend that before
integration,
        assimilation and mis-education

Before we 'stomped' to Kirt Franklin
and shook our booties to Mary Mary
quite contrary - *I just want to praise Him,*

Before neo-Negro Gospel Music,

Before Tupac, hip-hop, don't stop,
let me see who I can rip-off, rap music,

Before Jay Z, Master P, and P. Diddy did it,

Before BET, MTV, Fat Joe, sloppy Joe,
Big Tigger, Little Bow Wow, Crazy Rick,
Ludacris or just plain insane did it,

Before we overcame, there was
                such a thing called -
                          SOUL Music

But at 5 years old, Nyema didn't know
                      couldn't know
maybe even wouldn't know about it

Because teachers don't teach it anymore
Cooks don't slap on the gravy or bother
to put the "stink" on it no mo'

And Preachers don't moan like they useta
Don't scream "*Ohh LORD!!*" the way they did
during those home-going services
                that was such
                a foot-stompin'
                hand-clappin'
                gut wrenchin'
                soulful good time
                that even the caskets
                had to be tied down

Despite cable TV, VCR's, DVD's, and PC's, Nyema
didn't have a clue what her daddy meant when

he said — Soul, Baby! And she was fast-forwarding
toward —"I don't care daddy"

So how can I preserve our history?
Savor the black gold and tell our story?

I must admit, I was getting desperate
I've started screamin' like James Brown
Please! Please! Please! Please!

"Show me a sign Lord" I said
 a moan from Marvin
"*How sweet it is to be loved by you*"

 a holler from Jackie
"*The whisper getting louder*"

 a split from James Brown
"*Say it loud! I'm black and I'm proud*"

I said, "You gotta help me Lord!"

Next thing I know, I'm lying in bed
early Sunday morning
I hear vicious screams
coming from my kitchen
So I jumps up to see what it is

Now what it is - is the scream of a
tender-headed 5 year-old girl
getting her hair "done" by her
heavy-handed mama

I burst into the kitchen and said,
"Nyema, that's it! You got it!
"You got SOUL baby and you're super-bad!

Nyema stuck her thumb in her mouth, looked at me
and cried - "I don't want it daddy, I don't want it"

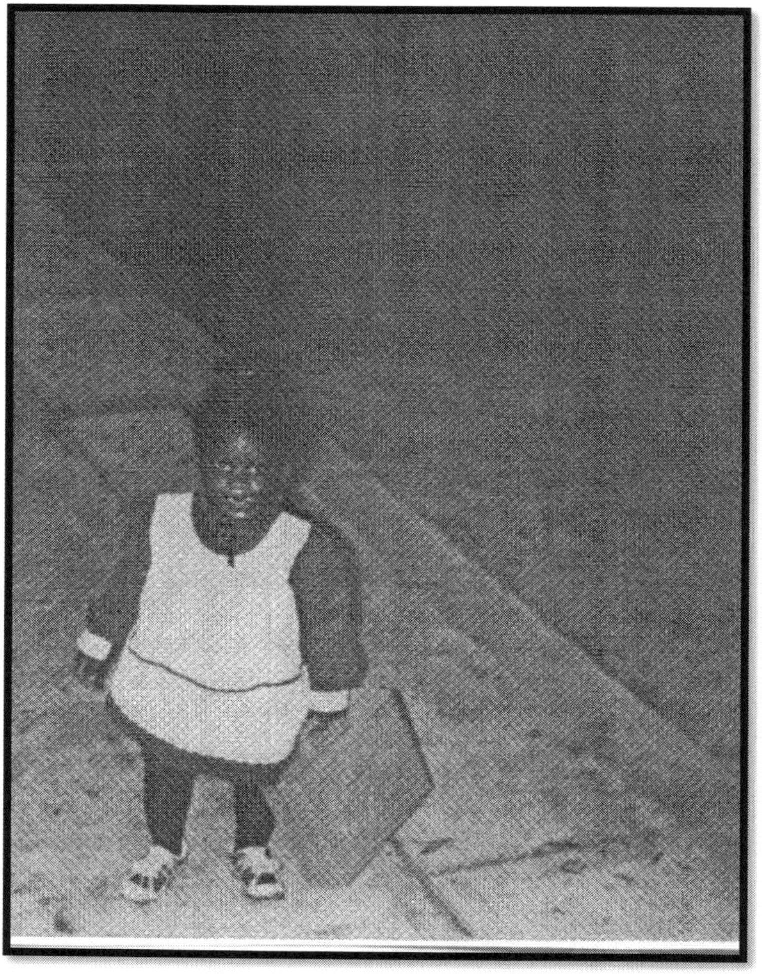

NO CHARGE

Mothers!!!
We all love them. All of us can identify with mom - right? She's the one person who sacrifices for us. Right from the beginning, a mother's love is bedrock solid. One popular gospel singer seem to say it best in her song, -"No Charge."

You see, it was mom who carried us for nine months with pain while we lived off her at no charge. After we were born, she fed and clothed us again at no charge. Through sickness and health, there was always mom. Whenever and whatever she gave us, it was always with love - but it was also FREE!!! It didn't cost us one cent. However, lately, mothers have come under attack from some very selfish, greedy and ruthless people - KIDS. Consider the case of the six-year-old who must have temporarily lost control of her mental faculties and demanded to be unconditionally release from her home.

"Ma," said the six-year-old. "I don't like it here anymore. I want to live elsewhere."
"Why?" Asked the mother
"Well, you're mean to me," replied the daughter
"Oh?" Said the mother
"Yeah! You don't give me as much money as Tiffany's mama gives her when she goes to school and you're always yelling at me to clean up my room.
"Honey, mommy loves you but sometimes I can't give you everything that other moms give their kids. And when I yell at you baby, it's not that I want to. Sometimes, mommy's not in a good mood. Will you forgive me?" the mother asked
"Um-Um" replied the little girl. I'm leaving. I'm going to live with Tiffany"
"Okay," said the wise mother. "When are you leaving?"
"In the morning," replied the six-year-old

The next morning, bright and early, the little girl arose. After eating a hearty breakfast, she proceeded to pack for her departure.
"Ma, where is my suitcase?"

"Do you mean *my* suitcase?" replied the mother, "because you don't have one."

"Can I borrow yours, ma?"
"Well of course you may, dear. But don't pack any of those toys."
"Then what am I going to play with at Tiffany's house?"
"I don't know" the mother said. "Perhaps you can play with Tiffany's toys."

The little girl seemed puzzled at a mother's behavior but she continued to pack.

"Be sure to pack plenty of underwear," said mom "but only one pair of shoes."
"I can't take my sneakers?" The little girl asked
"What sneakers? You mean the ones that I bought you last summer?"
"Yeah!" Replied the 6 yr. old
"No dear. Leave them here. I think I shall give them to someone who appreciates what I purchased for her."

Again, the little girl frowned at her mother's odd response but she kept on packing. About a half-hour later she emerged from the bedroom carrying a bulging suitcase, two teddy bears, a portable TV and a hangar full of clothing.
"Good-bye Ma"
"Wait a minute dear," said mom. "Let's see if you packed enough underwear. Everything should be nice and neat. Open the suitcase please."
"What's this?" She asked
"My piggy bank" answered the daughter
"Do you mean *my* piggy bank" said her mother. "I distinctly remember when I bought it."
 "And this looks like *my* jewelry, *my* slippers, *my* bathrobe, *my* tooth paste, *my* sweater, hat, gloves, skates, radio, deodorant, books, coat, etc.
"Ma, if you take back all these things from me, then I won't have anything to wear or play with at Tiffany's house except my underwear!"
"Well," said the wise mom, "have fun."

YEAR OF THE CHILD (1979)

Paid a visit to the hospital one day
and it came to my surprise
14 kids on a ward
Each one opened my eyes

They never knew
what you and I
seem to know
Dying old
is not so bad,
but dying young
and quite so slow - is very sad

It was on my mind in "79"

Jesse Thomas was just a little girl
Bright eyes, funny nose
long black pretty hair
She was very brave
and well behaved
But she wished she wasn't there

She asked my name
and wanted to be my friend
so I came to visit her
nearly every day
We laughed and we joked
right until her very end

In the corner
Little Ricky lays in his bed
No more crying
No more tears
I've started thinking about
some of the things
The Good Master said

"Suffer the little children
to come unto me
If you get into Heaven -
Thus shall it be"

It was on my mind and "79"

I counted 5 girls and 7 boys
with one set of twins
Some I knew would make it
But hope for others
was extremely slim

Preachers preach about it
Teachers teach about it
but who could prepare us
to deal with this?

Who could think about
countless babies dying
from sickness and hunger?
No reason to be bliss

Who could imagine
children losing a battle for life?

What part of humanity
should we give the blame?

What shall we do
besides cry out - what a shame?
It was on my mind in "79"

I UNDERSTAND
To Jackie: Once you know how, you never forget how to love

Think of me in no small way
For it is not menial, when I say

I understand

I understand when you're misunderstood
and your deeds go untold
When you labor bears no fruit
and your dreams start to fold

When you feel that you've done your best
and it is still not enough
When things get a little dark
and the going gets tough

Late at night when no one else hears
the sound of a restless pillow
and a head full of tears
Take refuge in me and still stand tall
because I understand in spite of it all

I believe in you simply
for whom you are

So believe in yourself
Step out and be unafraid
Be careful of doubts and misgivings
Don't be easily swayed

Riches and powers may brighten your hour,
Knowledge makes you wise
Beauty wins the prize

All these things give fashion and style
but they mean absolutely nothing at all
without love and understanding
once in a while

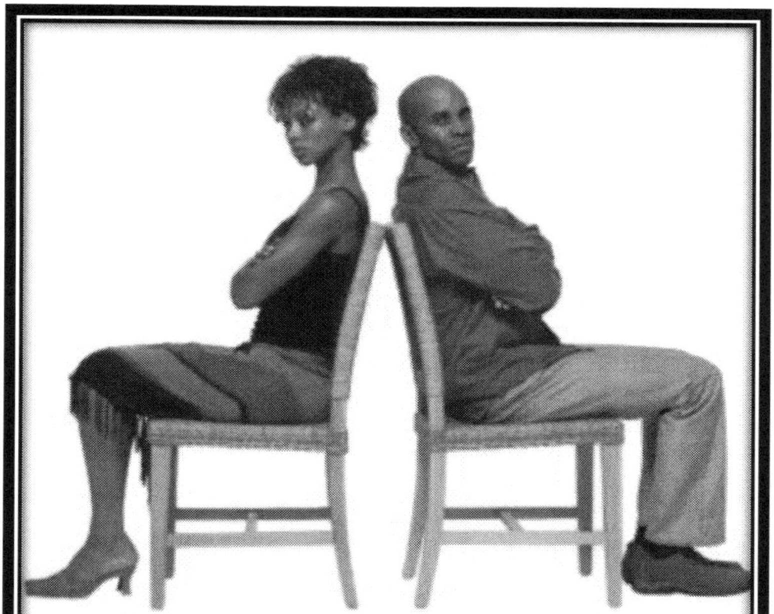

THE DEMISE

Brothers are blaming it
on the sisters
Sisters say —
"The brothers are uptight"
Blacks fault Whitey
But Whitey is pointing the finger right back

The have's claim it's the
have-nots who are causing it
But the have-nots are screaming
"They ain't cuttin' us no slack"

Negros down in the country say,-
"You breathe your troubles from the city's air"
But the urbanites reply,
"If we can make it up here,
Then - you can forget about down there"

All over the nation

Black families are splitting or being split up
like cancer attacking good cells -
They're under heavy assault

Despite the fact much of it is self-made,
they continue to pass the buck,
But the dichotomy is widening

It feels like someone or something
has just turned up the heat
But the B.S. keeps hitting the fan -
And is beginning to stink

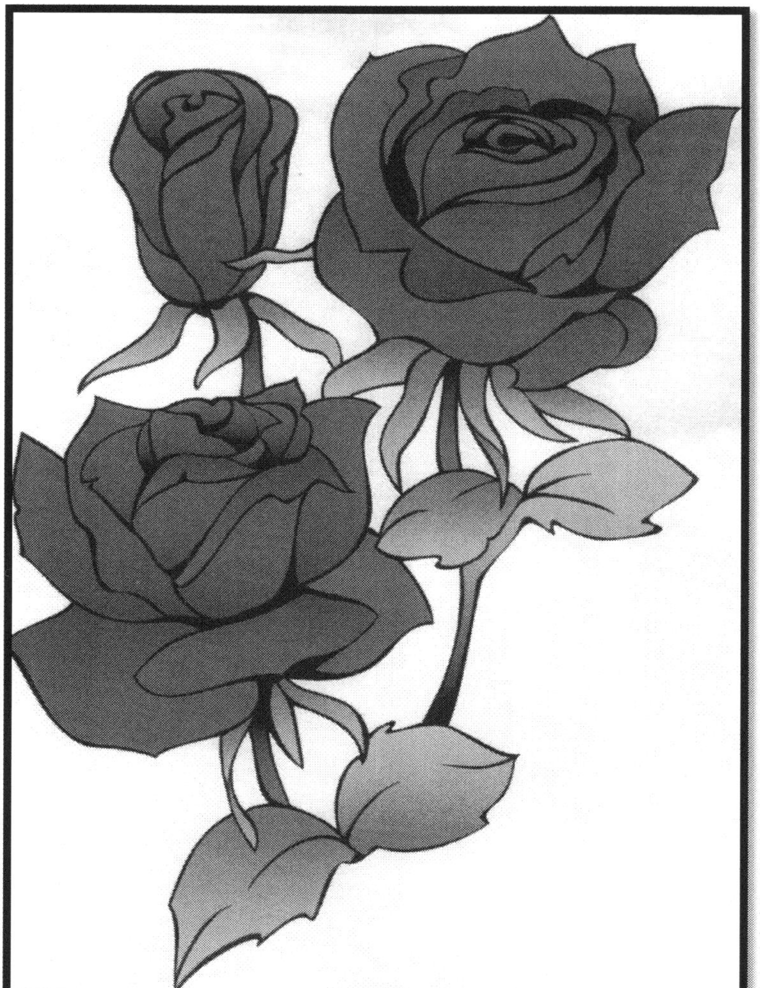

OUR FLOWERS

Our flowers don't unfold
The way we want them to

They bloom sometimes
unseasonably slow
Bending awkwardly to the left
or to the right

Seldom straight they go

It isn't often they know
the strength of their roots
or the elements that rushes in
to pluck their fruit
or suck their nectar
before their tender blossom's full

No, our flowers seldom
unfold the way we
want them to

They seem to test our love
Flaunting our faces
with their sweet fragrance
and hues so beautifully arranged-
Living only in the now

Heeding not our forecasts
of seasons change
Foolishly wasting their seeds
upon unsoiled ground

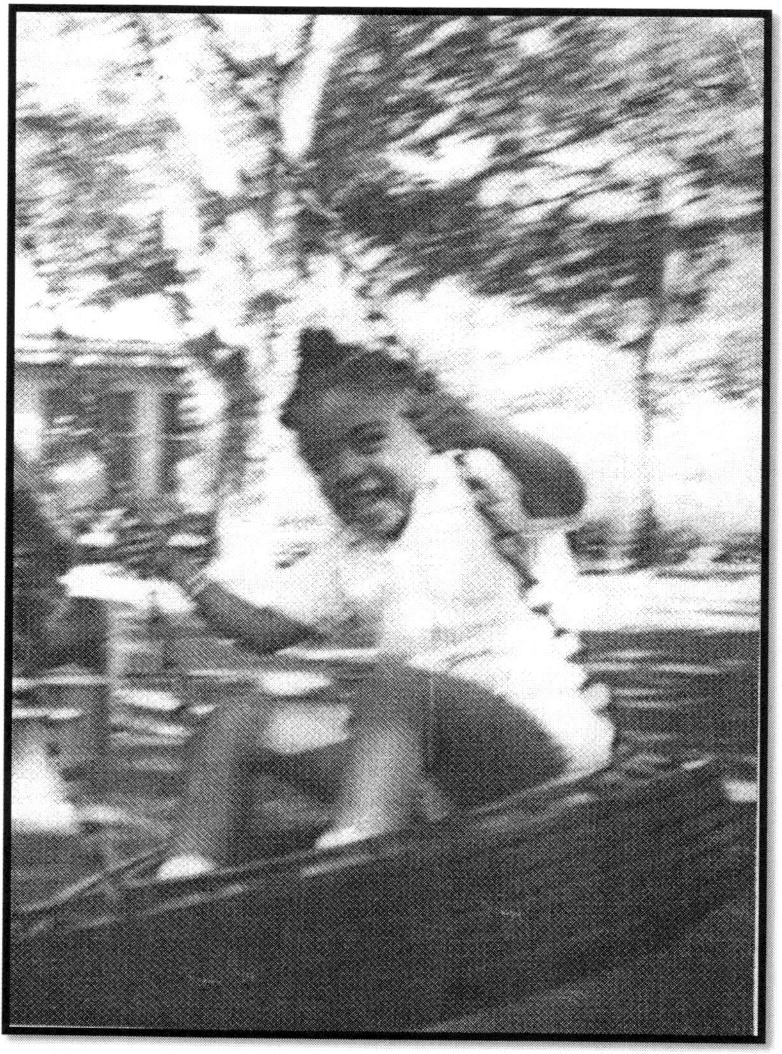

IF YOU DON'T PUSH NOTHING MOVES

The mission is not impossible

Good morning,
You are young, gifted and black.
But this may not be enough to save you.
Secret Intelligence has discovered a most clever plot to destroy your being.

Reportedly, enemy forces have penetrated your mind. A loss of identity and self-esteem has been observed. You are coordinated on a course of neutralization and should you decide to accept your mission - you will soon self-destruct.

In the entire universe, yours is the most coveted form. You are the most admired, adored, unique, and beautiful representative of life. There is none like you. No one feels with your compassion. No one moves in quite your fashion. Your movements are syncopated with the rhythms of life. In the sense that you were the first to introduce humanity to the world - you are life. Frequently, you will be emulated but never duplicated. You must be respected and protected. Any loss of identity, character or will to survive can inflict a serious blow to our future.

Without your signature, we receive no check.

Without your vision, there's a dream deferred.

Without you, there is no victory.

The phenomenon of future is strongly correlated with your survival.

YOU ARE THE FUTURE

Self-destruction is disguised in many patterns. It is the mutated gene with potential for unlimited harm that's growing in the cesspools of your world.

Before you reach the tender age of 25, you will have received 28,000 hours of nonstop subliminal racist media manipulation. A significant amount of your destruction will come from the music and images projected into your mind by misguided members of your own race via the cable, internet and other socially addictive resources.

Your destruction will be continually fostered by a xenophobic, sexist and racist institution, which systematically mis-educates.

You will have to take membership in yet another institution. This one will be known simply as - The Streets. It will have its own set of rules that will govern and control your behavior. If you engage in humanitarian, civil, social, active and meaningful protests, you will be swiftly incarcerated with little recourse for justice. Any childhood whim or prank will follow, and in some cases, precede you in an attempt to secure decent wages, housing and employment.

Under the guise of "competition is good for the economy," you will be pitted against your own women, people and race. They will attempt to convince you that language and nationality must take precedence over racial identity. In the final analysis, you will be trained to hate your family, your community your race, and yourself. Self-destruction will soon follow.

Do not accept the mission

Tomorrow can be the greatest day of your life.

You must not only dare to struggle

But you must push to survive because

If you don't push - nothing moves.

CARDS YOU'RE DEALT

Sometimes,
In life
The cards, which you were dealt,
Just don't leave you with an ace
And no matter how you try to hide,
It just keeps on statin' your case

Already,
You will born with two strikes against you
And for that you must take the blame

You gotta run this race called life
Though the startin' line
Ain't quite the same

You claim you need a break
Just to get you started and all
You say, you need a little help
Cause you're up against the wall

You live in a world
Where the odds are mounted up so high
That you ain't got a leg to stand on
And you think it's useless to try

But before you throw in the towel
And sound the alarm
That helping hand that you've been begging for

– consider the end of your arm

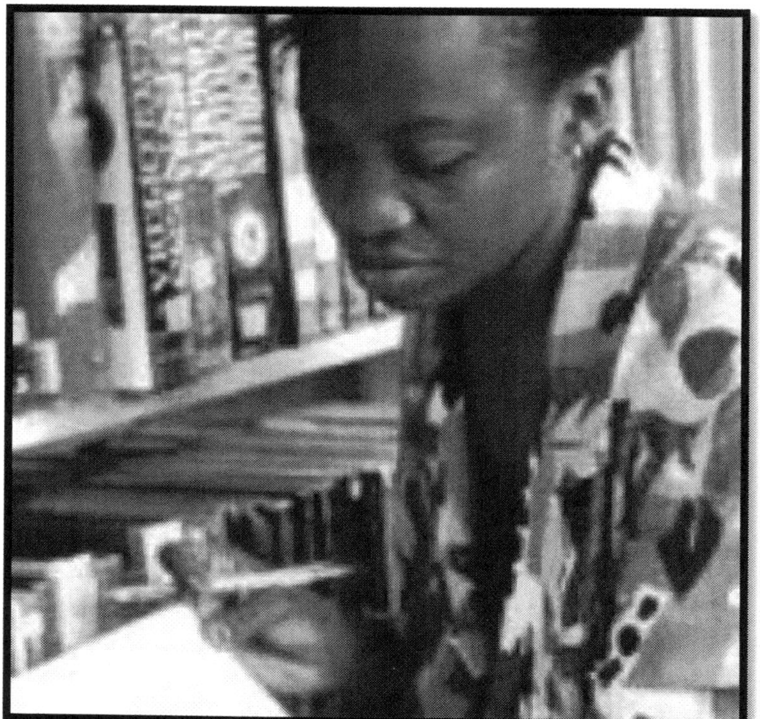

HATE DON'T MAKE NOISE

While walking through the library
quietly minding my own business
A book title caught my eye

It nearly blew my mind
as I thought about it a while
There was something different about it.
It had substance and a little style

"Just what kind of crazy title
for a book was this?"
I thought, as I poised
"What in the world could it
mean by hate don't make noise?"

"Hate don't make noise"
"Hate don't make noise"

I must've repeated this title
ten times to myself

Then, for peace of mind
I snatched it off the shelf

I started reading it when
suddenly it was clear-
This was someone's dissertation
Perhaps their private affair

But when I put the book back
the title kept ringing in my head
I thought if I had to title it
would I title it differently instead?

Does hate really make noise?
If so, what kind of noise is it?
Is it loud? Is it soft?
Does it sooth? Is it frigid?

All these things
I thought about
and yet, there was still doubt

You see, I had seen hate before
Thought I knew it well

I'd eaten, slept, worked and lived
with it and still, I couldn't tell
Does hate make noise?

I was no stranger to hate
Learned much of it in school
Ran from it Down South
Cursed it with my mouth

I bleached my skin
Curled my hair
Fixed my talk
and changed my name
because of it

My brothers in South Africa
call it apartheid. In America,
it was indigenous genocide
Yes, I've had more than one date with hate

Although I knew hate was around, after
all these years I didn't know how it sound

So maybe the first author was right-
"Hate Don't Make Noise"
It doesn't even bark
But one thing I do know —
it sure as hell bites!

WHERE DO WE GET THE STENGTH?

Where do we get the strength from?
Because we've been in a battle
Since day one
Whenever we challenge the system
For being unfair
When we fight our foes
And demand our share
Where do we get the strength from

How come we ain't tired?
After all these years
Why be inspired
When there's no ending near

You know there's still no admittance
They're holding us back
There really ain't no indication
That it's okay to be black
So where do we get the strength from?

We are always hearing
About the struggles in our past
About separation, segregation
The upper, the middle and the ruling class
But where is this strength coming from?

Since we can't convince the powers that be
To leave us alone or set us free
We better stay on the case

I mean it's hard enough
Just trying to make ends meet
Or hassling with the landlord
To send up some heat
But now your boss has got the notion
That you don't deserve that promotion
On account of the color of your face
Lord! Where do we get the strength from?

Folks don't realize
What it means to be black
They ain't sympathetic
And they ain't cuttin' us no slack

What they don't understand
Is we all ain't crazy
About collard greens,
Chicken and fatback

We don't all play loud music
Until late at night
We don't run like deer
And I declare,
Every one of us wasn't born to fight

Some of us ain't got no rhythm
We can't sing, nor dance and never
played the game of basketball.
I wish folks would understand that
black folks are just like everyone else
and what we really want is respect —
most of all

TONGUE - IN - CHEEK

So I'm watching TV the other day and I say to myself —
What kind of person goes to see a wrestling match?

I mean it's all right to read about it or watch it on free TV,
but coughing up hard earned money to see it in person —
what kind of fool would do that?

Just how much bull should we take before we say -
"Girl, I've had enough of this"

Not that I'm an expert or anything
but I think the best word for the battle
between Hulk Hogan and Macho Man is - "Tookin'"
That's the word my mama had for traveling salesmen,
love potions and midnight healers
Methinks some of y'all done been Tookin'

Oh don't get me wrong, I understand that sex sells.
When Jake the Snake shakes his behind, that *is* the bottom
line — I get it.

But I grew up when Bruno Samartino held the belt. Back
then, if you wanted it, you had to take it.

He didn't put your butt in a half-nelson then let you go
because you were the star of the show.
No - your ass was fully whipped

When new-age thinkers look at professional wrestling,
they can't be pleased. It probably reminds them
of the old Roman Coliseum
And I feel the same damn way

I can't stand to see grown men acting childish
with poppy-cock and balderdash spewing from their mouths.
Always talking about - "I'm gonna bust you up"

It seems to me, this could be the genesis to the
mindset which young boys carry into manhood

I mean what good is it for women and children
to be drop-kicked and body slammed simply
because some knucklehead can't separate the
hype from the reality or the sugar from the (s)ugar-(h)oney-(i)ce-(t)ea.

Ladies, must we be constantly reminded that what
we see is not necessarily what we get;
that push really doesn't have to come to shove
simply because some dumb-ass beer commercial
declares - "this slap is for you" or "It's Killer-Time"

Oh by the way,
When I say "just what kind of person goes to see a wrestling match?" I hope you understand that I say it in tongue-in-cheek because I was stupid enough to marry one of those kind.

Written in 1985

NEVER LET A MAN HIT YOU MORE THAN ONCE

They tell me, I - wears her big feet
                 shoulders her shoulder
                 and walks her walk
But I have yet to be told that I talks her talk

See, when you talk about bad English —
you talk about my mama
Folks forever laughed at my mama
But when they got through laughing - child!
My mama had what they call mama's wit
And it's a good thing I remembers it — good thing
Because you been walkin' 'round here smellin' yo-self lately
Do I needs to remind you that it was me who put you
                                 through yo schoolin'?
I don't know who you think you foolin'

Now that you a college man, some nights you get so smart
you can't find yo way home
But it's a pitiful, I say pitiful dog who don't remember
                 where he's buried his bone

Now, I ain't never been to nobody's college
but I didn't have to
'cause mama left me some wit too

Mama use to say —   "A pretty nigga is just
                         like a wild buck.
                         It be hard as hell
                         to harness his ego.
                         And if you get behind him,
                         he libel to kick you in de head"

                         "Girl! Neva let a man hit you
                         mo' den once!"

Last night, you done filled yo quota boy!

I'm on my way to work now
but before I leaves, I'm warnin' you
I done been in my closet
                and unpacked my mojo
When I gets home,
                both you and yo ego
had done better pack yo bags
You better be gone or so help me God – you be go!

And I'll meet yo soul in hell

THIS IS A LOVE POEM

This is a love poem, though it is incomplete
It has nearly all of the ingredients to make it rise
But if you try to sample it now, you may be surprised

This poem is seasoned with the imagery that we so cherish
in a love poem
It's cooked with sight
                sound
                    touch
                      feel
                        and
                            a distinct aroma of its own
But we should add something else to it

Love poems, like cakes, should be homemade-
We should bake them from scratch
They taste better when there's a rhythm
                            a voice
                              a tone
                                a beat
                                  a meter
                                    and a mood
                                      attached

When it gets to the proper temperature, we should add a bit of rhyme to it. While it's still cooking -

a little light alliteration	Love poems are like that
is certainly permissible,	Once you have the capacity
but a pinch of sweetener	to love, then you must
sprinkled on this contents	wait for the right
makes it truly medicinal	cooking conditions
Things tend to happen	That is why this love
for two basic reasons -	poem is not quite
Capacity and Conditions	done.

It needs one more condition before its ready.
Perhaps it's waiting for . . . . .

WHO WROTE THE RULES?

Who wrote the rules?

Who said that wrong could never be right?
Who said that yesterday is gone forever -
And I could never feel exactly what I felt then?
Where is the person that has done this?

By what authority?

Who, what, where and why did they
write this rule?
Without my permission
Who said that everything must change?
That I am changing; my hair is now gray -
My skin, my teeth, my bones are changing

Who said wrong could *never* be right?
Was it right - the life I lived?

Who wrote the rules, tell me?
Where can I find this person?
So that we can talk
So that I can tell Him that wrong is
Not always wrong,
And right is not always rightfully so

And before you write another rule,
Understand that in the case of a living
Human being

There is a SOMETIMES

HOW DO WE SAY GOOD-BYE?

How do we say goodbye? How do we do it?

Why do we say goodbye?
>Birds never say goodbye -
>they simply say so long
>but we'll be back again
>Flowers close shop for the winter but
>leave us a note of hope
>that spring is just around the bend

So why do we say goodbye?

Out of all God's creatures
we are the only ones where
goodbye is more than just a season

Yes, the good die young but no -
we don't ever know the reason
So how do we say goodbye?

Where does sorrow get the nerve
and who are we that we deserve
to be treated this way
>In all of nature, it's so unnatural
>the way we say goodbye.
>Flowers don't weep
>and birds don't cry
>So why can't we be like birds and fly
>south in the winter of our lives -
>avoiding the sadness, sorrow, misery
>and strife of saying goodbye

Wasn't it yesterday we played on the playground?
Didn't we skip to the loop, peekaboo and dance
around the merry-go-round?

Such pain we bear when we depart!
Beseeching sorrow to release our hearts

So how do we say goodbye?

Sorrow knows the answer, yet conceals
It does not want us to know
that unlike the birds that fly
and the flowers that grow
buried deep in our soul
there is unspeakable joy -
                We are the only ones made in
                His image and likeness -
                In Him, we live and move
                and have our being

Yes, there is pain in losing our loved ones but in
truth, they're going back from whence they came

Here's the secret that sorrow doesn't want to reveal
              - "To be absent from the body
                Is to be present with the Lord"
                Because Earth has no sorrow
                that Heaven cannot heal

NIGHTINGALES

Nightingales could sing about it

                                  But they won't

Ashanti Drums could beat their sweet rhythms

                                  But they don't

Picasso could paint it
Shakespeare could write it
And a single candle could light it
                                  But it doesn't
Egyptians could built it
Martin could march for it
Gandhi would fast about it
And on top of Mount Everest
We get all shout it
                                  But we don't

Architects would design it
Explorers could find it
Experience would teach us
And Venus could reach us

Why! We could rewrite history
And the universe would yield
Its deepest mysteries
                                  But it simply won't

Every one of them waits for you and me
to really mean it when we say — Peace, Be Still

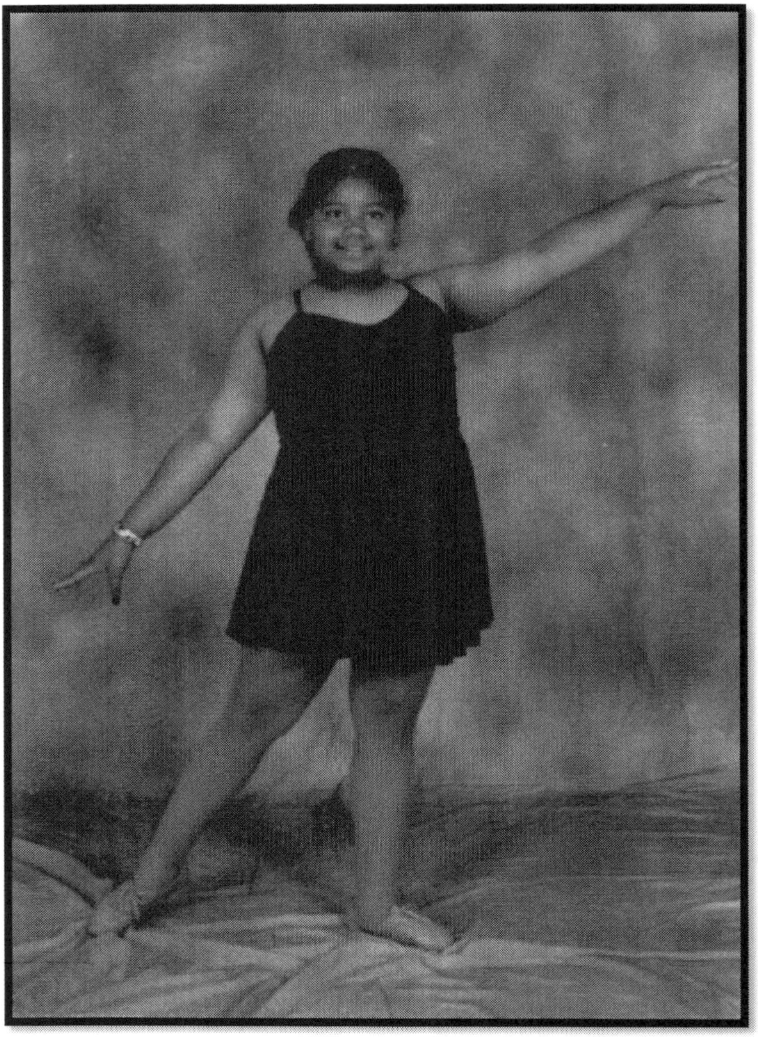

I COMMISSION YOU

My darling little niece
As I walk through the ghetto
I know something that you don't

As I watch you and the other
children swing to the beat
of the latest tunes on the radio

As you dance in the streets
and giggle out loud so
comfortably in your world

I know about the rhythms that
are bottled up in your soul
but cannot be suppressed
I see it leaking through
like blood dripping from
a badly bandaged wound,
refusing to cover the pain
or, camouflage the damage
that was done
I know about Africa

But I also know about the blues
that grieves your mother
As a single parent, your mother
works awfully hard for you

I watched the sweat run down
her face, alluding the wrinkles
that identify the struggle she's in

I watch as she returns home from
working overtime, double time and
sometimes triple time on your behalf
I see that there is nothing she wouldn't
sacrifice or spare for you
There is nothing she has not denied
herself for your welfare

The endless nights of fatigue
wears on her body like make-up until
it becomes too difficult to wash off

The imageries, thoughts and concerns
for your future lines up in her mind
as an army of soldiers would,
awaiting the call of the battle cry
Is there anything too good for you?

Every time she turns on the TV,
opens a magazine, views a show,
hears a speech or sings a song —
She sees you
You are the reason for existence

My darling little 13-year-old

While you insist that she gives you
money to purchase the latest jeans,
While you beg for stylish shoes
and cry for additional "hangout" time,
your mother succumbs to the
fantasies of your growing pains
But in reality, she longs to give you
something else for your troubles
Something of substance

The identity that you so frantically
search for in your dancing needs
to be cultivated
The nuts and bolts of your machinery
have to be greased
After all - it is you who must break
the psychological cycle of pain
You are the future and this is your world

My darling little niece
You must dance!
Dance my darling!
Dance as far as possible

Pirouette until you shake loose
the shackles from the ankles of
Africa to the fruit of our labor

Kick the dust off the soil
of your ancestors
Jump across the oceans of
despair that divides us all
Dance!

Shake the ground and rattle
the dry bones of the dead
Hurdle the obstacles
that bind our brains
Dance away the pain
Dance!

So that someday
your mother and I will sit in
the audience of a well-orchestrated
performance of yours
And while the audience applauds,
we will weep the tears of joy

I know that your movements will liberate us

It is for this reason
my darling little niece -

I commission you to DANCE!

THERE'S A RHYTHM TO LIFE

There's a rhythm to life
If you get in step
There's a steady beat
Once you let it flow

You may not always feel it
Because it's soft
And it's low
But there's a rhythm to life

When the wind is at you back
You can sail the breeze
Once you pick up the feelings
You can move with ease

Life has a pulse that never stops moving
We must respect it
Or endure its tribulations
But if you can get it together
There is a rhythm to life
And it's giving off sweet vibrations

CALM DOWN

Calm down my brother
Don't let it ruffle your feathers
Don't let it still you
Try not to dwell on the damage that was done

Fix your mind on a quiet ocean breeze
Blowing across the waves - and move
Move yourself to a higher plane
Rise above the rain

Calm down my brother
I know how you feel
I know the truth

JUST A TESTIMONY

This is just a testimony
to let you know
God made the sun
to give us warmth
and brighten our day
He made the flowers and trees
that are beautiful and gay

He's provided the earth, the air and the sky
The mountains and the valleys He freely gives
All that we can eat and drink is fully supplied
so we I may live

All these things give testimony from God up above
Courtesy of the Almighty, from Heaven with love

But take time to notice there is no label
Saying "Made in Heaven" to show us He's able
No sign that reads - "Made by God"
or signature saying "I've Done My Part"

You just have to notice that
everything is already in place
There's no unfinished business -
nothing incomplete, nothing unsafe

This thought of abundance brings me to you
Because you're beautiful too
But take time to notice that you too wear no label
You don't have to advertise for me to see you

If you share your smile with me,
It will be a testimony —
that you're still in love me

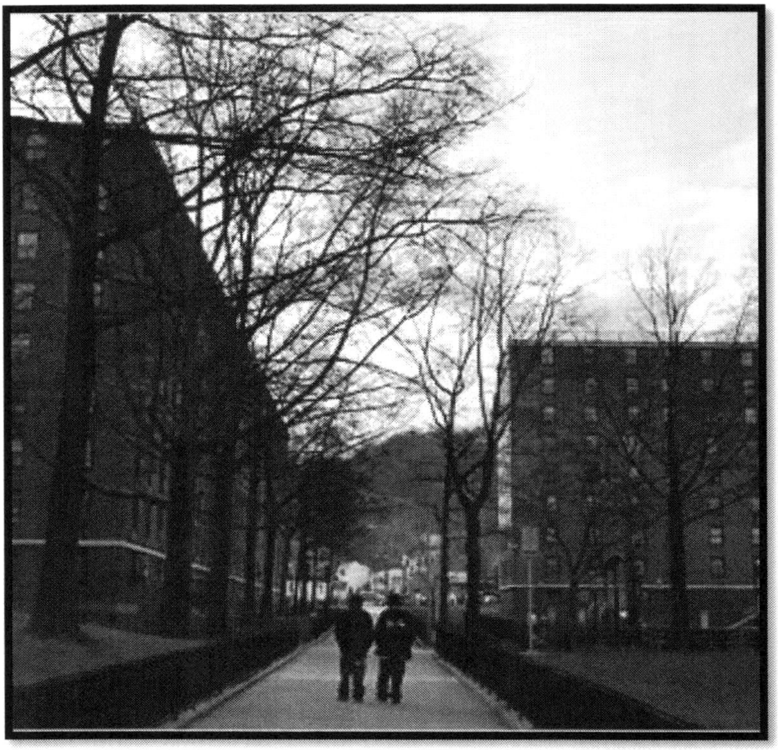

JESUS CHRIST WAS A SOCIAL WORKER

Politicians, preachers and image makers
have a propensity for reducing everything
to three levels - black vs. whites
                God vs. devil
                        Democrats vs. Republicans

They like to set the ground rules
draw the borderlines
and control the tempo

You either play by their rules or,
like some spoiled child,
they take the ball, pull the plug
or stop the game

But when Jesus comes,
they won't recognize Him
Because He won't be in all the usual places
where celebrities gather -
                    Though He is The -"Star"

There won't be any film at 11,
cameo roles or curtain calls
You're not going to find Him strolling
down Hollywood's Walk of Fame,
Ripley's "Believe It or Not"
or dancing in La Cage Aux Folles

Tell Congress Jesus won't be joining
them to address the best method of
convincing the Russians to be reborn,
nor will he accept any social invitations from
the President to sit and chit-chat
over cocktails and hors d'oeuvres
on the White House lawn

No - look for Jesus in the Harlem's, Watts
and El Barrios of the world.

Look for him in storefronts, log cabins
and country shack churches. In hospitals, prisons,
nursing homes and senior citizen shelters

He'll probably be wearing a beat up coat, blue jeans,
T-shirt and an old pair of Adidas

He'll be eating chicken, collard greens and hominy
grits - living in a public housing project,
or perhaps playing basketball

Throughout history, He has always been identified on
the side of the oppressed
because Jesus was a social worker - most of all

NO COMMENT

Does the Black Church have anything more to offer than chicken dinners, fish fries, building funds, broadcasts, BMW's and Lexus's?

Is there anything else they can do besides singing, shouting and begging for our souls?

Are there any other sins besides gambling, gossiping, lying, sexing, smoking, drinking, pornography and short skirts?

Black folks are some of the most religiously dogmatic people in the world

So why don't more black preachers preach more to white sinners -or don't they sin too?

Black people, in general, have difficulty figuring out what to do after they are "reborn." So many of them conform to "getting high on God" or just having - "church!"

Whatever happened to the church's commitment to combating unjust institutions of the world?

Since Jesus never attempted to divorce himself from the political and social issues of his day, why does the Black Church dismissed this part of his demeanor?

Among other things, Jesus was a mover and shaker, a disturber of the peace - a troublemaker

But many black preachers must have a section or chapter in their Bible they call the Fifth Amendment. Because every time they get an opportunity to speak on a social or racial issue that affects our lives, they say what is in effect — "No Comment."

UNSUNG HEROES

Dedicated to Rev. H. L. Williams,

This one is for the unsung heroes
Those who are un-bought and unsold
Who gave their blood, sweat and tears
down through the years
Yet, whose story has never been told

This is for your unsung work
after the celebration was over -
but the struggle had not quite started
Here is the credit you've never received
for all of the values you have guarded

Although it is not enough for
the many years you have given,
nor the pain that was driven
by the harvest that you reaped

There simply is no fitting tribute
of alloy, metal or gold that can
repay you for a job well done
and a spirit, which ran so deep

But, we humbly say, "Thank you"
though we're a few generations late
We will never renege on your deeds
for we are committed by our fate

While the world looked at Martin and Malcolm X -
pondering the question - who will be next?
There was no mention of YOU - as if they acted alone
No mention of the sacrifices you gave,
nor the lives that were saved or the
tremendous courage that was shown

So this one is for YOU

Who marched in back of the crowd behind the scene
where there was no exposure, cameras or press
No film at eleven or stairway to Heaven
But still, you gave us your very best

Because God uses ordinary people

You were a plain old ordinary guy.
But oh, how you tried to right the wrongs,
which plagued our lives!

You protested with sit-ins and boycotts
Sometimes there was violence, sometimes not

When you turn the other cheek,
you found out that it hurts just the same
Some of you were beaten over the head
and even some of you are dead
But your dying was surely not in vain

It was YOU who carried the weight on your
shoulders for US - saying, "We ain't gonna let
nobody turn us around"

You have made this world a slightly better place
for all races to live in, still, you do not wear a crown

              YOU ARE AN UNSUNG HERO

And the moral arc of justice is long
there was much need for - plotting and planning
                              marching and standing
There was much need to be strong

Though we hate to look back, you took us from
Negro to Black as you cried out - "We shall overcome"

But if somehow we overcame
it's ridiculously a shame
how quickly we forget where we came from

How soon we forget our history
and the people who made it so
The real people responsible for our progress;
the unsung heroes that far too many of us —
just do not know

CHAMPION

I don't always feel like a champion
I'm not always victorious
Sometimes I feel defeated
Other times I'm not so glorious

I know that I must appear
invincible to many
But when I'm all alone
my tears come aplenty

All my life, I was oh so strong
with vigor in my eyes
And even now, God knows!
There's nothing in me that wants to die

But I'm lying on my back
Wounded by a most clever foe
Wounded not by bullet, by knife,
by arrow or bow
Not of a hunter, a soldier, an animal or
any manner of man who stalks the night
But of one who disguises himself
as a member of my own kind

He accompanied me on many a journeys
I bestowed in him an element of trust
Together, we had a physical relationship
free of envy or lust

Yet, it was him who betrayed me
and left me powerless to defend
Still, I'll never confess my weakness
I'll be champion into the end

He skillfully attacked my body
and oh so swiftly I fell

Let it be known that
I fought the good fight
but was defeated by the one
called Sickle Cell

RUMOR-CONSUMER

There's a rumor
about the consumer, which
must've begun on the outside

        It claims we're naïve
        in our choices and we
        select with no pride

Word is out that
our lack of education
has stunted our upward mobility

        The constant apathy for how
        things are the disrespect for
        the powers that be

We must pick ourselves up
by our bootstraps - learn
to take the bull by the horn

        We must prove ourselves fit
        before the breakage of
        a new dawn

We simply haven't excelled
because we lack the will to work
hard to become successful

        This is the logic they
        propose to people who've
        been oppressed

Though I cannot validate
this rumor - it's not for
me to say

        But the truth is -
        It's so unnecessary
        for us to live this way

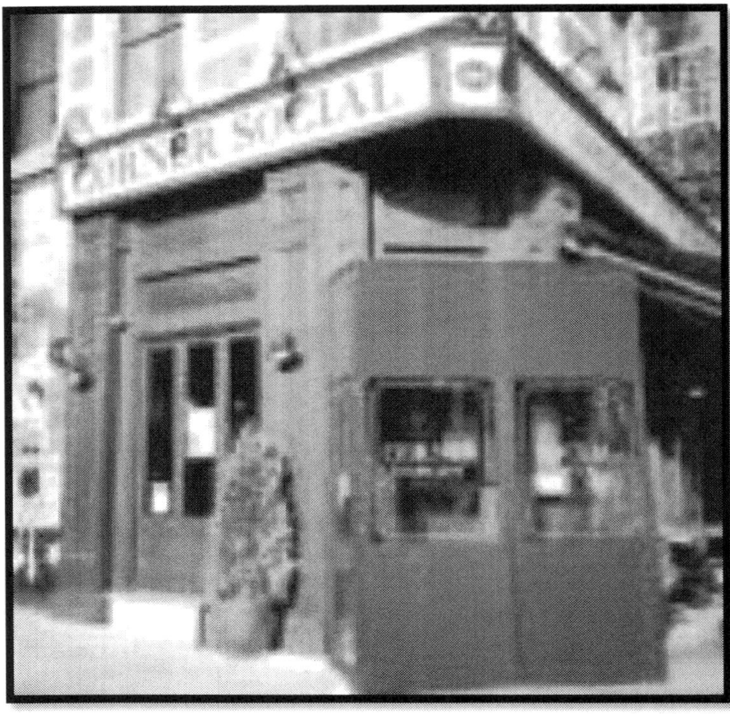
CORNER SOCIAL

MEMBERS ONLY/HARD TIMES FOR LOVERS

Burning with passion, he walked toward the door of the sleazy club and softly rapped three times on the door. "Are you a member?" said a sexy, smooth voice from behind the peephole.

"No, I'm not," he replied.

"Well then, it'll cost you 25."

"25! All that just to get in?" he said.

"That's right, my friend. This joint is for members only."

"Well, what do I have to do to become a member?"

"She said, slide 25 under the door honey, then come on in and let's talk about it."
He reached down into his sock, pulled out the money and slid it under the door. When the door finally swung open, a tall sultry woman smiled and said,

"Now, sugar, what's it gonna be?"

He said, "You don't understand. This is an emergency."

She said, "I've heard that line before."

"No, first I want to see what you got." He replied.

"See what I got? Fool! You lookin' at it! This ain't no John's Bargain Store. You can't be samplin' the goods."

"That ain't what I mean. I just want to get straight and I know what it takes."

"Well, honey, if you don't like me, there's others in here that can do that. But don't be wastin' our time. You ain't some kind of freak, are you?"

"Why would you say that?" He asked.

"'Cause you looks to be the kind," she answered.

"No, I ain't no freak. I done told you, I just come here to get straight!"

"Alright! You don't have to get so testy." She shouted. "We got to be careful you know. There are all kinds of germs out there, including A.I.D.S."

"I know what you mean, baby, but I use my own equipment and I never share."

"Oh, you're into the personal touch," she said, smiling. "I'll tell the ladies to beware."

"Ladies!" he said, "you got ladies in here too?"

"Of course we do. We don't be mixin' the sexes in here. No sir, we ain't got nothin' but girls. I knows these are hard time for lovers but ain't that much love in the world!"

He said, "Hard time for lovers? I didn't come here for no damn love! I needs me a fix."

"Fix, what kind of fix?" She probed

He replied, "The kind of fix you put in your arm, stupid."

"You go stick your stupid-ass mammy in your arm, you little bug eyed bastard! I knew when I opened the door for your little pitiful butt, I'd be getting in a mess."

He said, "Ain't this 1106 Hampton Street East?"

She replied, "No jackass! This is 1106 Hampton Street West. Now you get the hell out of my place!"

I WILL

Give me chance -
          And I'll supply reality
Offer me hope -
          And I'll produce triumph
Let me see today -
          And tomorrow will be delivered to your door
Show me uncertainty -
          And it will surely be controlled
Sell me what you perceive to be the end -
          And I'll purchase a new beginning
Serve me a dish of what's wrong -
          And I'll season it with what's right
Pour me a cup of life that's half empty -
          And I'll drink from one half-full
Bring me desolation and dismay -
          And I'll send them away
Contaminate my vision -
          And I'll bathe in a dream
Just try to put me under - And I'll rise above your rain

AIN'T NO SUCH THING

Mosquitoes on the wall on a hot summer night
Better kill them now, lest they bite you good
when you turn off the lights

Ain't no such thing as leave it alone

One house on the block on fire
right next door to 10 more
Nobody's walkin' up the block screamin' -
"Hey! What you puttin' out that fire for?"

Ain't no such thing as leave it alone

Heard a preacher man preachin' last Sunday
He say, "Anyway you fix it up - sin is still sin
And it's sho-nuff sinful iff'n you're gay

Ain't no such thing as leave it alone

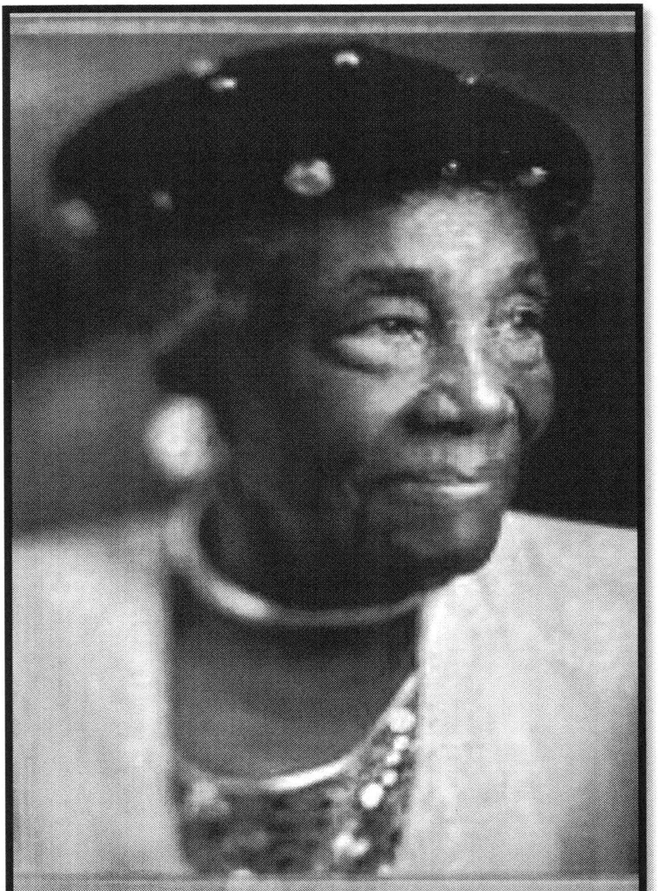

MOTHER REARDON DRINKS A LITTLE

I, Mother Reardon, drinks a little
That's right! Furthermore - I'm just not a shame

'Cause when you've gone through
what I've been through in life
Honey, you needs to little bit
just to e-e-e ease the pain

Now, I ain't hurtin' nobody but myself
Yet, you'd be a fool to think that I don't know it
Whereas one time I was good and strong
I tell you that my nerves are gone now
and my hands are startin' to show it

You see, I'm getting o-o-o-old now
But that's not what's troublin' me so
I ain't studyin' these wrinkles on my face
'cause I believes when you gets to be my age
they just spose to show

But there used to be a time,
when I was a young and foxy,
All - I say all the dudes would come around
They'd come around all dressed up,
slick and sassy right on down

And it wasn't too long after that,
one of those dudes caught my eye
Honey! That man was so good looking,
the girls would whistle when he walked by

You know I hooked him!
We got married and soon started raising
another beautiful young man
It was too bad that he had to die
in a stupid and senseless war
ways off in some foreign land

Oh but nevertheless, I done live me the good life
Most of the time it was just my old man and me

We ain't never did nobody no harm
and on Sundays, a-sittin' in church we'd be

Yes, but I'm getting o-o-o-old now and I finds
those saints don't come around much anymore
I suspects it's 'cause I can't tip that ole offering
plate like I used to, Um-hmm!
That's just why they ain't knocking on my door

Ah! But it's just as well 'cause I can't
get a grip on myself, as they say
I ain't been myself in years -
not since my old man went away

You see, he laid down with me one night
and did not get up the next mornin'
That man died in his sleep
without no word, no sign or no warnin'

E-v-e-r since that time
I do's my best just to carry on
My friends tell me that I looks good
but in my heart I knows I'm just not strong

You see - I DRINKS A LITTLE! That's right.

And every night before I go to bed
I takes me one good l-o-n-g swallow
and prays that in the morning —
they finds me dead

TOUCH BASE

This One –
Is for old folks
Cause there's nothing like
Feeling what they feel

Nothing like having your
Grandmamma dry your crying
Eyes while she's rocking
And holding you tight

It's a real good feeling
To a three-year-old who's
Tremblin' with fright

This One -
Is for my dear Aunt Clara
Who's so sweet in gray

T'ain't a thing in this world
Like hearing us say
"Stop by after school today,
I've baked your favorite pie."

This Here -
Is for old man Jenkins
Who likes fishing
And sitting down by the banks of
The river just shootin' some breeze
Nothing like those lazy summer
Days - taking is slow, taking easy

Old Sam Willis tells the best damn
Stories from here to Timbuktu!

*Legendary stories, about legendary
People, of whom he claims he knew
Don't matter much if he stretches
The story a wee bit. After 10 times of
Hearing the same old story,
I'm still not tired of it*

*Old folks in general
Come from a different generation
Different notions and different ideas
But the same meanings*

*This one-
Is for those of us who like
To touch base with them*

*To listen to their sound advice
To seek the expertise
To share our thoughts and deeds
And discover their needs*

*Some folks believe that old folks
Are gonna make it somehow
Come high waters or low
But just like the song says -
"It ain't necessarily so"*

LET THE STRONG HELP THE WEAK

Let the strong help the weak
When they fall in despair
Let them offer their strength
And show how they care

Let the mighty be there
When the light has grown dim
When joy has turned to sadness
And hope is wearing grim

Let the Blessed be compassionate
And deeply concerned
Showing wisdom and guidance
And giving in turn

When illness has claimed the body
But not the soul
Let them heal
The grieving spirit
And make it whole

When death has raised
Its ugly head
Causing heartache and pain
Let the strong bring in the sunshine
Driving back the stormy rains

And when their own strength
The strong cannot sustain
Let them call forth
to the Source
And lift his Holy Name

WAIT

Did you ever stop to think about all of the things in life that we wait on? Here are just a few of them

We wait on   we wait for
buses and subways   night times and right times
vacations and holidays   mornings and afternoons
pensions and paychecks   sun times and fun times
that we must collect.   that cannot come too soon
Tax returns and raises
to which we never say – "what the heck!"

We like to wait on such important things as:
Luncheons and dinners   papers and mail
   Losers and winners   babies and maybes
     Pennants and playoffs   lovers and mothers
       Hitters and payoffs   juries and judges
         Products and sales   gripes and grudges

We wait on sunrise and sunset. The spring and the fall
On doorbells, door rings and important telephone calls
We wait for fuel and for gas, to follow and to pass-

We love to wait on
movies and books   horses that race
food that cooks   success to taste
hair to grow   forks and knives
knowledge to know   husbands and wives

          We wait, we wait and we wait

We wait for bruises to heal   There are doctors and lawyers
and drugs to ease the pain   that we all wait on.
we feel. Government red   Bills and laws
tape that we must go   that take so long
through. Rules and   Industries, companies
regulations - some old   wine and cheese;
and some new   clothing, records,
                              flowers and trees

With all these things in life that we tend to wait on -
Why is it so hard to wait on God?

HEAVEN IS

Heaven is a place created by
the fourth dimension of your mind

It's a place that's out-of-sight
It's together
It's sublime

Heaven must be where God is
and also His Son
But what if you finally get there
and can't find either one?

Still, some folks sing about it and call it by many names
They live their whole life to get there, or so they claim

But Heaven really is hip

How else can we climb so high without ladder or rope?
How else can we open our mind without synthetics or dope?

Heaven really is a place created
by the fourth dimension of your mind

No one has ever returned from it to give us the big scoop
No one has ever told us about its molecular breakdown
or the chance that it's a fluke

The only thing they say is Heaven - is light-years away

So did I hear you say you want to go there?
Heaven bound?
"What's the best way to get there, you ask?"

Tell me. What does your Bible Say?

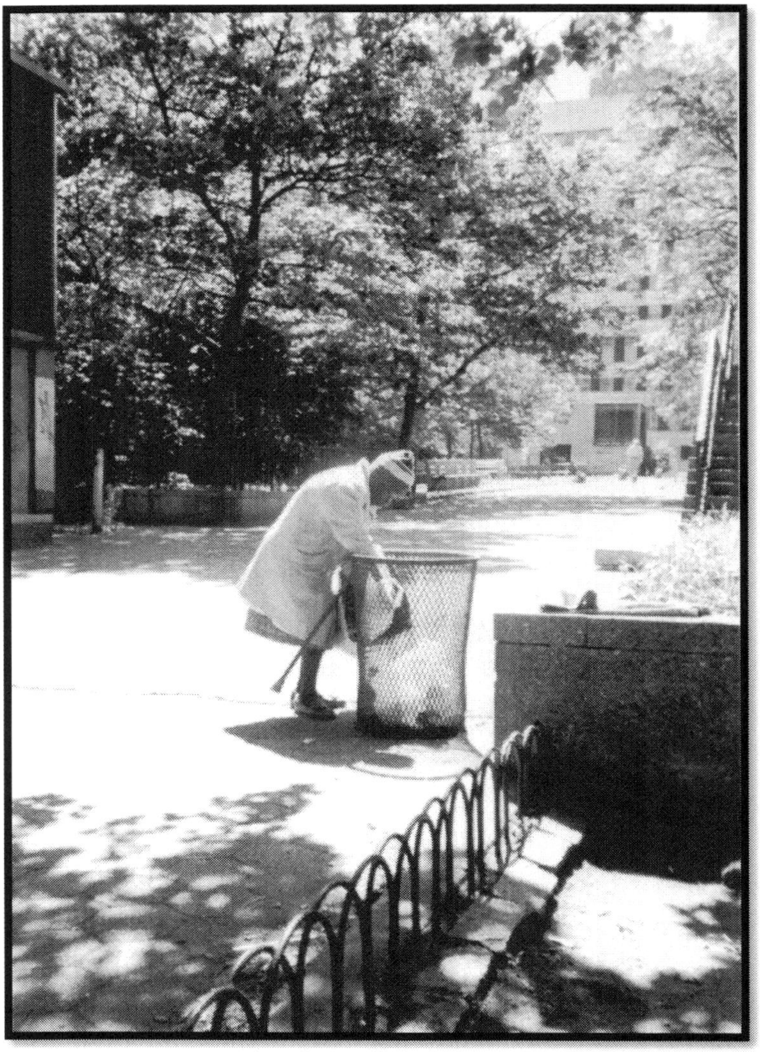

TELL GOD WE NEED HIM DOWN HERE

Tell God we need Him down here

Sin has broken loose
And gone off on a tear
Jumped in the waters
Shaken up the seas
Climbed up the mountains
And kicked down the trees

What was controllable
Has now gotten out of hand
Thanks Satan and
the wisdom of man

We are scared to death
From the air we breathe
So, come right now Lord
We're ready to receive

We fear for our children
In a world that's not safe
We're praying for their future
But we're losing our faith

Tell God we need Him down here

Because mankind
Has not been kind and all
It is threatening destruction
With nuclear warfare
Building up weapons
Like it just doesn't care
We're dying for reasons
Which remain untold
Sickness and disease
Is still unfold

Death is lurking
With needles and dope
Claiming young lives
And leaving no hope

Old folks are hungry
Eating out of garbage cans
Living in the streets
Without pot and one pan

Many are scared to walk
The streets at night
Locking their doors,
Trembling in fright

Women press their way to work
Just to make ends meet
But when they come home
They're robbed in the streets

Tell God we need Him down here

Some say -"We are living in the last
Days. The Scriptures must be fulfilled"

But I remember how you calmed
The waters of a storm-tossed sea

How even the winds and
waves obeyed Thy Will

I believe everything will be alright

If you would only say, "Peace - BE STILL"

NO DEPOSIT – NO RETURN

What is it that's sandwiched
between a dream and reality?
Successful people know
hard work and discipline
is the same it seems
whatever you do, wherever you go

Life is an endless stream of choices
and over its cliff many are falling
So let us not choose to lose, but hang up
when self-pity starts calling

Whenever he's serious
there's nothing nefarious
which blocks an achiever

It gets rough sometimes
but inside of his thirst
there's strength for the journey
and tea for the fever

Betwixt and between ideal and the real
there are principles we must condone
There comes a time to remove life's
training wheels and balance it on our own

Life will teach us many things
and many things we will learn
But none more important than
No deposit – no return

Between bereavement and achievement
there has never been an ocean
You may reach success by chance
But it is far more likely
it will come from your devotion

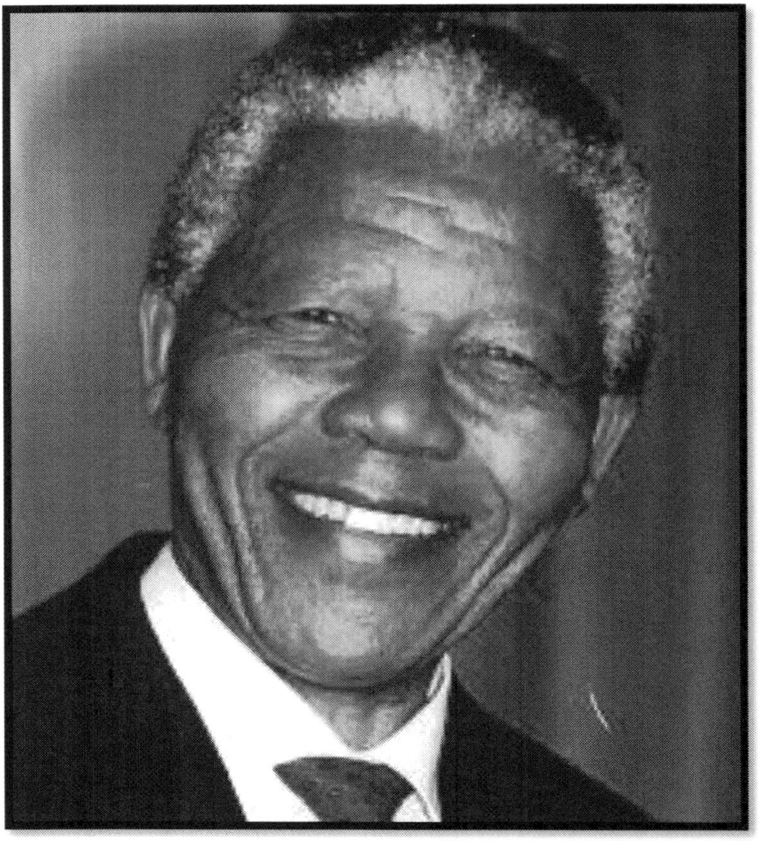

BE UNCOMMON

("*Nelson Mandela is a hero*")

He was born an ordinary man
under sub ordinary conditions
but somehow, he rose
to extraordinary heights

Two roads diverged in his woods and I,
        "I" said Nelson Mandela
        "I chose the one less traveled
         and that has made all the difference"

This world belongs to an uncommon man or woman
So let us be uncommon for it is our right to be uncommon
                                              - if we can

A great man named Henry David Thoreau once said,
"If a man does not keep pace with his companions,
perhaps it is because he hears a different drummer. Let him
step to the music which he hears, however measured it may
be" - BE UNCOMMON

Another great man, Dr. Martin Luther King declared,
"Be a bush if you can't be a tree, but be the best bush that
you can be" - BE UNCOMMON

Life is an endless stream of choices
but over its cliff, many are falling -
so let us not choose to lose when self-pity starts calling
Because Longfellow was right!
"The heights by great men reached and kept,
were not attained from sudden flight,
but they, while their companions slept ,
were toiling upward in the night"

"If you can keep your head about you" said Kipling,
"While others are losing their and blaming it on you
If you can believe in yourself when others doubt you
but make allowance for their doubting too
"If you can fill the unforgiving minute
with 60 seconds' worth of distance run-
Yours is the Earth and everything in it
but more than this, you'll be a Man my son!" -
BE UNCOMMON

And if you wish to be like Nelson Mandela
and live in a universe of adversity -
Where you're common dignity was routinely denied
but somehow keep your integrity
If you can face brutal unkindness and suffer not
the disease of "possibility-blindness"
but say to yourself – "I AM SOMEBODY!"

If you can get knocked down
and not be so defeated
that you no longer wish to try
If you can see your problems
as a God-ordained opportunity
cleverly disguised as an obstacle
for you to rise up to meet it
If you can take life's broken wings
then you could learn to fly

If you can withstand the pain
of being a 50-year-old man
but your name is still - "boy"
If you can govern your tongue
and discipline your disappointments
without losing your joy
or your historical mind

If all that you dream and scheme is about it
and life seems useless and worthless without it
It may take 70 years for you
to hear the words - "well done"

But if you can do it, "Yours is the Earth"
and every God-blessed thing that's in it
But more than this, like Nelson Mandela,
You're gonna be a man, my son!
BE UNCOMMON!

I ALWAYS WANTED TO BE SOMEBODY

I always wanted to be somebody
        wanted to read about me in magazines,
                see me on TV and
swear every word I say - was a tribute to me

Ever since I was a little nappy headed child
I dreamed about getting ahead
Not the head of my class
but the stratosphere

I wanted to fly so high - no one could reach me
                wanted to soar like a Star

I just wanted to be somebody - no one in particular
I wanted to cover myself in adulations
        adorations
        and acclamations
All day, every day
I dreamed about me 'til I was were spent
Dreamed I was a deity, or at least Heaven sent
It's all about me 'cause I always wanted to be somebody

I wanted ABC, CBS and NBC to fuss over me
Wanted to dictate to the president
To tell Shakespeare what to write
Ali who to fight
and James Brown, how to get down -

Wanted to swing with Cab Calloway
            sing with Aretha
            and croon with Marvin

Can't you just see me in a ticker tape parade
with homemade humility
Yeah! I can too

I see me on the six o'clock news
on Dallas and Dynasty
even Hill Street Blues

I'm running the bases at Yankee Stadium
    selling out the Palladium
and getting a standing ovation at Radio City Music Hall

I just signed a 10 year mega million dollar contract
and I'm on a worldwide tour with
                16 movies featuring my name

There not one
but two of my feet
planted on Hollywood's Walk of Fame
'Cause I always wanted to be somebody

I can't watch another movie or TV show
about the Rich and the Famous
Don't care who just hit the lottery for a zillion

All I care about is my burning desire to be somebody

I know I'm trippin' but do me a favor?
Don't pinch me! - Not yet

Written in 1986

WHERE DOES THE SEA END AND THE SHORE BEGIN?

Is there border between a myth and a lie?
If you can't always tell the difference, neither can I

Who decides what is beautiful and what is art?

Be careful of people who say their life is ideal
Watch out the kids who insist Santa Claus is real

There are still people who wonder who built the pyramids

How dark can a person be if you like him tall, dark, and handsome?

How far can someone let himself go before pleasingly plump turns into just plain fat?

Does the Bible actually say Adam and Eve ate an apple?

Who talks funny - the folks Down South or the folks Up North?

When does curiosity cross the border to simply nosey?

Is the word "androgynous" more acceptable than "weirdo?"

Can "socially comfortable" be a code word for racist?

Should we apply the term "terrorists" to the European invaders of Native Americans?

OTHER SIDE OF THE TRACK

There is no difference in me from you
I come from not only the same
side of the track
But like it or not,
the same street too

In the mornings, as we
to commute to the city,
We stand on the same track,
ride the same train,
bust our butts,
then bring it on back

If there is a difference
maybe it's the fact that I give
my brain a rest at night —
in the form of sleep
so I can meet the man the next day

While the fiendish, childish boy
in you stay up late at night
plotting to rid yourself of me —
Saying "let me count the ways."

LOVE IS LOVE

Birds tend to be birds
Fish can only be fish
Trees are just trees

Water flows into water
Air dissipates into air
Flowers are flowers
Horses are horses
Snakes are snakes
Dogs are dogs and
Sheep are sheep
but LOVE

When you think about it
LOVE IS . . . .

PRIDE AND HUMOR

*One John Doe
Used to laugh
when Mary Jane strutted her stuff
It pleased him well!
Now he no longer thinks she's cute
Due to the fact - his love fell*

*There was once a sense of humor in him
And Mary felt free to kid around
Now, she holds back her feelings
She's tired of being put down*

*Their once hot and juicy relationship
Has somehow gone dry
John's feelings for Mary have changed
Though sadly, Mary continues to try*

*She has only one thing left -
and that is pride
Nothing else she can brag about,
Nothing left to hide*

*When it has finally leaves her,
she will count the pain
as the days go by
And while she's doing that -
she might as well count his lies*

*Cause his pride and humor has left
They're the last two barometers
of a dying affair
The last two indicators
that he just doesn't care*

CONVERSATION # 1

                Some people like to take refuge in one-liners

"Hold this bottle, man. I gotta take a piss."

"Hey man, why I gotta be yo trash can, throw that bottle in the street. Ain't no mo' wine in it anyway."

"Yo dog! Bust out with the herb and let's get down."

"Nah, bro, I'm savin' it for bus. I wanna get the whole damn bus high!"

"Yo, dogg. Look at that fly bitch over there across the street."

"Ooooweee! I sure like to bust that out. She walkin' this way too!"

"Excuse me, any of you brother got a light?"

"What you seek is a match sugar, cause *I AM* the light!"

"*Say what?*"

"That's right, baby. You talkin' to the Light - I'm God."

"What makes you think you're some sort of God?"

"It ain't what I think, it's what I know - I'm God and you're the earth. You feel me baby?"

"No, I don't feel you. And let me tell you something. I'm getting a little sick and tired of all you young brothers walking around here talking that dumb crap. You need to stop frontin' and get yourself together."

"What you comin' out your face for, bitch! You don't know me"

"Oh I know you brother. I see your kind every day. And you have the audacity to think you're somebody's God. God wouldn't go anywhere near you. Squeezing your funky feet

into a pair of stolen sneakers, bragging about how many times you've been to jail and grabbing your crotch every time some woman passes by don't quite qualify you to be God. You ain't no God. You're not even a man yet.

What kind of God disrespects women, neglects his family, rips people off, smokes dope, drops out of school and lives off of the government?

If you really think you're some sort of God then you're suffering from a rare form of stupidity."

"No brother, you ain't no God."

"At best, - you're just playing a big game with yourself."

NO ONE NEEDS TO FEEL INFERIOR

No one needs to feel inferior
No one human

You'd think we'd know that by now

Cats are not inferior to fish and
fish are not inferior to birds - they just are
        All of God's creatures - just are

None of them are born wanting
to be something they're not

There's no innate need to be black or yellow
                      or white or brown
Neither a need to be smarter than the average bear

The only need a baby cares about is a nipple to suck on
                      a chest to lie on
                      and a shoulder to cry on

It doesn't have to best anyone to
prove its superiority or Darwinism
The question of whether it is fit to survive
has already been answered by the Creator

So there's something to be said about people who
        are always closing doors
           erecting walls
           and raising quotas
People who segregate, separate and eliminate
lives to make space to call their own

Whatever happened to the principle of live and let live?

People, who carve out exclusive corners of the earth,
        rope off private continents and post
           "Keep Off" signs on the beaches of God's
        Green Acres are like teenagers quarreling over penis
        supremacy

Does anyone really need to have a "First," "Second" or
              "Third" world label attached to their race?

Does anyone need to be told their hair is too short
                                    eyes to slant
                                      or nose to wide?

You shouldn't have to tear me down to build yourself up

I hold these truths to be self-evident that
                                If I am cut — I'll bleed
                                If I'm pleased — I'll smile
                        and If I am young — I'll dream

No one is compelled to feel inferior - no one

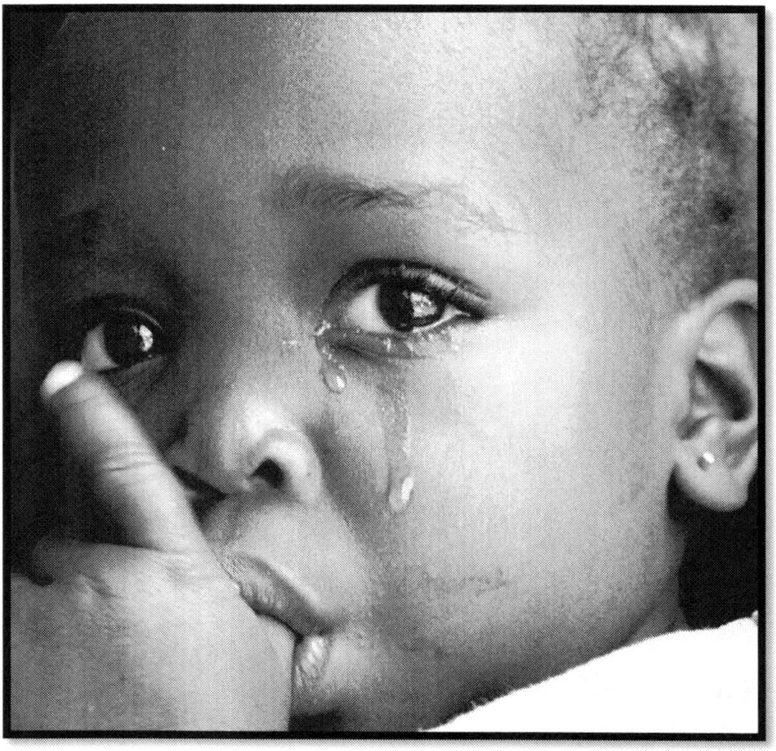

SUMMERTIME

*"Summertime and the living is easy
fish are jumping
and the cotton is high
Your daddy's rich
and your mama's good-looking
So hush little baby Don't you cry"*

Maybe, it's because I see your needs waiting while paying customers are serviced first

Maybe it's the 24 hours of nonstop hunger
or the discomfiting stench of two day-old
pissed-filled Pampers but I find myself singing —
                    '*Summertime*' and
                    '*God Bless the Child*'

Perhaps it's the beauty of that paint-chipped
                    lead-filled
                    colorless
                    nursery of yours

Or could it be the camaraderie of the rats
and roaches that you've befriended
or perhaps the love for you
that was *never* intended
But I tremble and shake
when I think about what they're doing to you -
the helplessness, hopelessness and unabashed
degradation they're putting you through -
Child, somebody thinks the world about you-
so hush!

You were unexpected, unwanted and unplanned, but well-rehearsed. Could've been anybody's child, anybody's mistake, But somehow you missed that slaughterhouse they call the clinic and you ended up much worse — unloved.

I call you my summertime baby 'cause for you, living ain't gonna be easy
Normally, flowers are crazy about sunshine

       spring adores rain and
          sorrow is tickled pink for joy.

Ordinarily, the sun rises in the East,
birds fly south in the winter and
the priceless presence of a newborn baby
is a joyous occasion
But I'm sorry to tell you —
          No One Is Celebrating Your Birth!

There has been a change at the network
for maternal reality. All programs
broadcasting normality has been pre-empted

No darling, your daddy's isn't rich - he's in jail
And there he shall be for the next 25 years

Due to her allegiance to the almighty crack pipe
your mama is no longer good-looking
She's just out looking for someone, anyone to spend
the night with -
to get it on with
to get down,
to get high
and get out before sunrise

Crack has got her sprinting
but she's unable to go the distance with you. You're
no match for the crystal rock diamond that refuses to
shine, so hush -up!

Don't you dare plan on sucking her breasts tonight.
Some other sucker has beaten you to it.
She calls them your uncles but I don't think so
See uncles don't get it on with their sisters
They don't exploit them for sexual favors
or steal their money
Don't use terms of endearment
like "do me baby" or "stroke it honey!"

No child! They ain't no kin to you
Now hush! I say hush, dry your cryin'
eyes and let me explain

You see, it was never intended that you should
suffer from benign neglect.
But neither your mommy, nor daddy is standing
by your side - it's not your fault
      In another time, another place
      you might've made it
      Your mother would've been a
      Queen and your father - a King
      The whole village would have raised you

> *"But it's summertime*
> *and the killing is easy*
> *Crack is popping*
> *and the business is good*
> *Your daddy's gone*
> *and your mama's out tricking.*
> *So hush little baby - nobody wants to*
> *hear your cry!"*

I SEE THE WORLD

I see the world through a crystal colored ball –
a ball that is forever turning

I see it as a spiral staircase moving upward
And every step I make is a step of learning

I see it as children do,
through a glass window pane
One that's untainted,
incorruptible and unashamed

Though my world rotates on its axis
It's really a multi-dimensional sphere
A sphere sprinkled with spice and beauty
with a little adventure
and a whole lot of flair

I think of it as a carousel
going round and round
from side to side

And if you've got a nickel in your pocket,
the next time it stops,

Jump on board and take a ride

YESTERDAY'S CHILDREN

Written by A.H. Reynolds

i

Heavy knitted blue
        covers nose/eyes/ears/head
white soiled rag conceals
        the aperture of desolation

darkly buttoned wool hides all but shoeless feet
one meticulously wrapped, - one meticulously bear
                aside propped on
painstaking pasteboard print
explaining his plight but never
        touching
        on his true
        condition
    "MY NAME IS BILL
    PLEASE HELP ME"

ii

with right hip bone in right hand
and chest meeting chin
she delves into germ laden leavins,
collects aluminum off the streets
        a dollar by the hundred

    "welfare say they caint he'p me
    no more 'cause *now* I got me uh *job*"

Dignity that forages
    wired mesh and
    rusted bins for gold
knows the gruesome touch
    hard times can hold

iii

black/ brown /green/gray lumps of consumptive waste
spew from the throat
desperation/splatters granite walk ways looking on

a cold sun brightly mocks the struggle to subsist

HARD RAIN
(Written in 1985)

Something is about to happen

Call me a prophet, but something
is soon going to happen

What is about to manifest
has never happened before
Nevertheless, many people
will surely be ready for it

It's been a long time coming
But in a country where apartheid
rises with the sun —
A hard rain is gonna to fall

DISSONANCE

Since you're able to do both
Whether you should tie your
left shoe first or your right
Given the choice, it doesn't matter

Whether you should vacation on
the Riviera or in the Bahamas
Given the choice, it's no big deal

Because you can do both, whether it's
- Coffee   or   tea
  Coke   or   Pepsi
  Stocks   or   bonds
  Houses   or   condos
  Mercedes or   Porsche,
  It really doesn't matter

But as the earth revolves around the
sun and the problems of the so-called
Third World begin to affect you,
whether you should laugh about it or
cry about it - is really up to you
But you cannot do both

MUTUAL

"Mutually," said the sorcerer
"I am not what you perceive me to be"

I am here!
You are there!
You are there and I am here!

Don't you see! Don't you see!

You may come!
I may go!
You may go and I may come!

OBSERVE me, and then quickly extrapolate.
But Hurry up!
You have only a moment then it will surely be too late

"For time," said the sorcerer
"Is the only thing that I do not have"
All wisdom, all knowledge is within my POWERS
The universe, the sky and the mystery of the stars

I touch! You feel!
We both exist.
"But only you are real," said the sorcerer

In my world, I must constantly change.
Else, I shall cease to be. So it is!

Don't you see! Don't you see!

In your world, there is equal time given
For all, there are 24 hours. Yet I
I must change, my friend - lest I lose my powers

At night, we differ only in the twinkling of an eye
But in the morning, like magic, I MUST say good-bye

Don't you see! Don't you see!

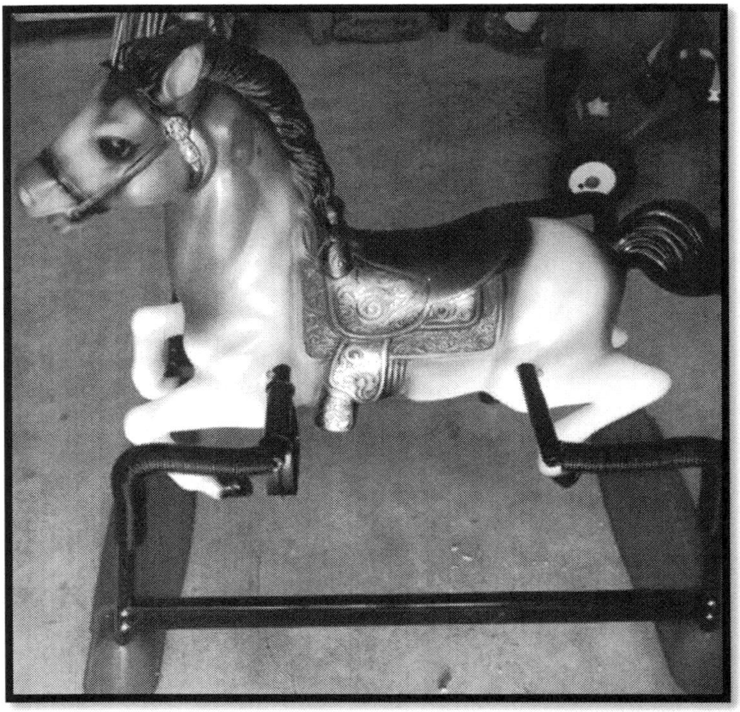

KINDERGARTEN MEMORIES AND PAINFUL REMINDERS

The room is filled with pictures, artifacts and memorabilia. There's a bicycle living there, a rocking horse that still rocks and a very famous mouse

Lincoln Logs are all set up and ready for play. One thousand soldiers await their command and will eagerly obey

There's a fire engine with movable parts, roller skates, a slinky toy, a shiny red wagon and a closet full of storybooks to warm your heart

They are all here - *kindergarten memories*
and painful reminders
when living was easy
and life was kinder

Multi-colored gifts of endearment
like alphabets and fancy shapes
are covering the walls
and coloring the drapes

Rectangles, triangles, squares
and circles secretly hidden
inside old spelling words

Animated animals meticulously named
A desk, a table, and a rocking chair
that no one has claimed and oh yes!
A funny looking fella named - Big Bird
They are all here - *kindergarten memories*
and painful reminders
when living was simple
and life was kinder

In an old house
stood an old man
reminiscing about yesteryear
and his only son -

"Boy! I don't think you know
how simple things like a kiss,
a card, or an airplane made of
paper-mache use to brighten my day"

"How many times did I hear you say
'I made this one for you daddy,
do you like it?' Then I'd say -oh I love it!
Let's hang it where everyone can see"

"How often would you remind me
to lock the doors at night
You'd say, 'Remember daddy, before we
go to bed, we got to lock the monsters out'
And I'd say, "oh yeah, ain't no
monsters comin' in here tonight!"

Watching you grow up
was only half the fun
of watching you glow
Your innocence could brighten
as bright as the sun could shine

Why, I remember the time you ran
all the way home from school
huffin' and puffin' as you burst
through the door "Daddy! Daddy!

The teacher gave me a special star today.
She said I was the best example of what good
behavior is -Are you proud of me daddy? Are
you proud of me?" Then I'd say —"boy!
I'm as proud of you as proud can be!!!"

You use to be my sunshine
My bright and shining star
But you've gone and changed boy
I don't know you anymore
They tell me my son is
a big-time gangster now

They tell me - if you need
anything, you're the one to see

But I could never be proud of you
'cause I didn't raise no gangster
Your mama's gone now
and I'm still holding on

Stop writing me letters
Stop sending me checks
I don't need your money
'cause you ain't my son no more

The sweet little boy
that I once knew
left me a long time ago
And all that's left of him are these —

*Kindergarten memories
and painful reminders
when living was easier
and life was so much kinder*

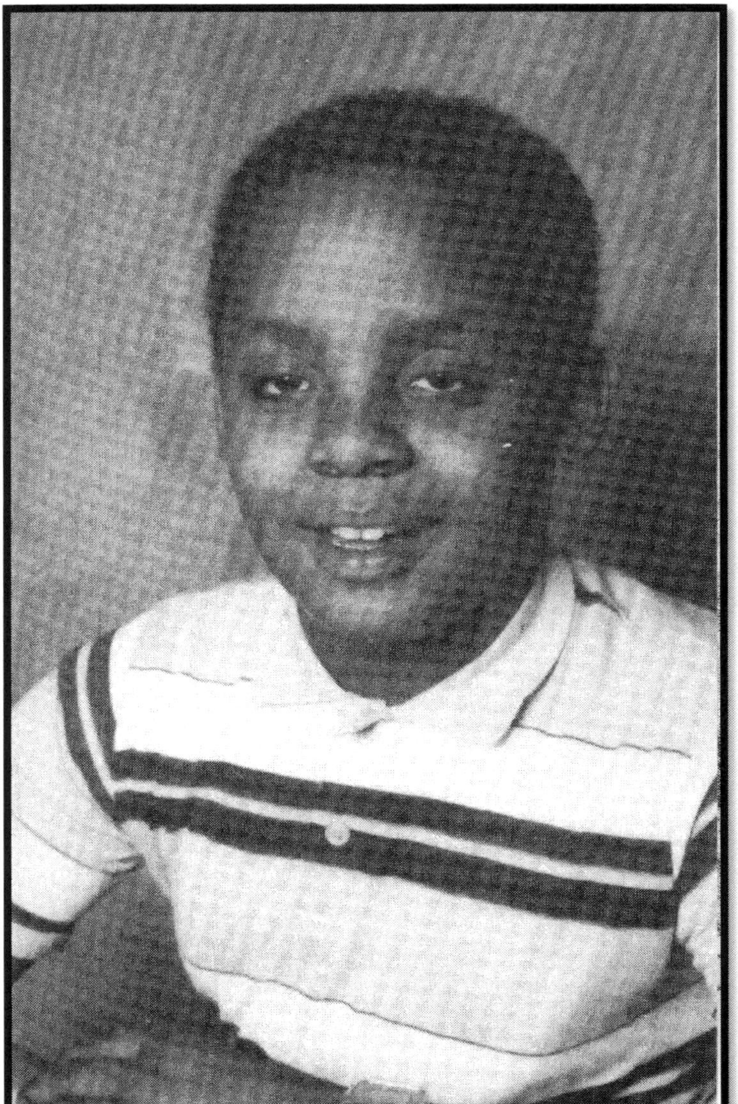

COMING INTO HIS MANHOOD

He's 15 years old and still very much unaware of what it means.
Missing gloves, skelly tops, and wax candy whistles appear to be
no longer in his repertoire. He seems to have a higher agenda

He ain't got no mindfulness of
the dangers that be shadowing him – No
He don't know nothin' 'bout no shaky ground he walkin' on.
He just be floatin' on a cloud of play

But I say, whose job is it to check his footin' anyway?
I always tells him, "baby chicks and street tricks
comes a dime a dozen in this neighborhood" –
cause they do!

But no need to worry much 'bout the baby chicks.
When time comes for them to leave their nest,
they be's fully equipped

But my child ain't no man yet and I aims to keep it that way
15 is awkward age enough - all by its solitude
So I says,
"No thanks" to the extra troubles that comes with it

He's a strong boy. But the streets be stronger
I see dope, crime, and the police get the best of them.

Got no mind to squeeze him
but I can let him stretch too much either
'Cause I knows that freedom can make you self-destruct.

When he wants to go outside, I tells him it's all right. Yesss -
it's alright - 'cause truly, he done been covered under de blood

But I still can't seem to relax
No - can't get no rest while he is gone
Not 'til I hear the key turn de door

CUM BY Y'A
(Come by here)

"Cum by y'a, my Lord
Cum by y'a
Cum by y'a, my Lord
Cum by y'a
Cum by y'a, my Lord
Cum by y'a
Oh Lord, Cum by y'a"

This is a "Cum by y'a" time we're living in
Folks are taking every opportunity to prove that
They do, about as little as they can
And then - no more

So every time I open a newspaper
or turn on a TV
and hear about some poor
mother's child starving to death
I say - Cum by y'a
      Cum by y'a, my Lord,
      Cum by y'a

Folks living on the street as
vagabond's and shopping bag ladies
need not be subject to further ridicule —
oh but they are!

We give them nasty looks and dirty gestures
then say to ourselves, "such a waste"
But is it really fair to judge another woman's life
when all the pieces of her puzzle are not in place?

There's really no need to look at another
person's failure with humor or fun
Life is a holistic experience and trying to make
something out of it is easier said than done

When we measure another woman's life
We'd better measure it well
We can't look at it as if it was
simply some grammar school test
which maybe she failed

No - we've got to take into account
all of the personal hills and valleys
She must've gone through

We've got to look at the battle scars
from the struggles she's been in
Scars that were cut so deeply
They're no longer visible - but the pain is still there

This is why I say - *Cum by y'a, my Lord, Cum by y'a*

We want you to come by here - Right Now

WHAT'S THE WORLD DOING OUT THERE?

"What's the world doing out there?" Hubert asked "Because I don't have to open my eyes; I could just lay here in the friendly confines of my mind. So, what's the world doing out there?"

"Do you really care?" asked Monty

"Sure I care," Hubert replied. "That's why I asked."

"Well, if you really cared, you'd open your eyes and see," said Monty. "You take a good hard look at what's happening and begin to act on what you see."

"Yes, but I don't have to," cried Hubert. Morning's dawnin' and I'm still yawnin,' so I don't have to open my eyes if I don't want to. No, I'm going to stay right here 'til somebody else takes a good look and tell me what the world is doing out there. Dis here cardboard bed I'm lying on is bound to become more card-board-ier and dis here sheet that's quite so wrinkled is gonna get tinkled cause I ain't gettin' up."

"You'd be a no good lazy guy," shouted Monty

"You ain't got no gumption, no sir; not one damn drop of gumption in you and therein lies the shame. 'Cause you ain't got no gumption, you won't even try."

"But if it makes you feel any better," Monty answered. "I'll tell you what I'm gonna do. "I will look out there and see what the world is up to - except *Now*," said Monty, "after I tell you, you're gonna be acting on what someone else told you and not what you saw with your own two eyes. You'd be acting out what little gumption you might have on something that could just be a Great Big Lie!"

TO HIM THAT WOULD BE GREAT
Dedicated to Roy King

You have not achieved greatness
until you've learn to be the least

He that is great should not
narcissistically approach life,
nor produce the ruins of vanity
Rather, he should struggle to
sustain a course of righteousness
and be the best that he can be

Great men endure
life's on-going struggle,
though it brings with it much pain
They break the dawn of a new day
while others are walking in the rain

Greatness does not shed
when trouble draws near
It doesn't run from adversity
for in it dwells no fear

It is most evident when it's
offered in the form of sacrifice
For there is no greater love
than he who lays down his life

To him that would be great

You will treasure memories
of yesterday's gone by,
but prepare for tomorrow

You will weep dearly
after losing a loved one
But swim not in your sorrow

For every experience in life -
there is significance
Each end brings forth

*a new beginning -and
this is how it must be*

To him that would be great

*Your course of greatness has
been set in motion a long
time ago by One who is even
greater than you*

*Struggle not to free yourself
from the responsibilities at hand
If you fall short of victory
Continue to be a man*

*Respect your women
Treat them like Queens
Stick around to see your babies grow
Share and their hopes and dreams*

*Though you must laugh sometimes
when you're compelled to cry
When denied the dignity of work
you will continue to provide*

*When others take but rarely give
It's your task to be compassionate
but your character to be sensitive*

*Because greatness is more
spiritual than a state of mind,
when it is finally achieved-
To him that would be great*

You are truly one-of-a-kind

TERRITORIAL BEHAVIOR

O-pened-up
a psy-chol-o-gy
book one day

Star-ted read-ing it
my own kind of way

That's when I ran into a phrase
called "Territory —Behavior"

It meant -*people acting strange
in a certain geographical space*
Then suddenly I realized
They were jumpin' on *our* case

In a sneaky sort of way
what they were trying to say
was *we are* acting abnormal

Who else could it be
when they say -
*People acting strange in a
certain geographical space*

Although they call it a case-study
they surely did lie
It was a study of *our* case
because we were snatched from
our land in an experimental
group to see if we could adapt

We were put in a cage called
America to run a course
Ran so damn well
we were reinforced
and still, we must take the rap
of "Territorial-Behavior"

The procedure was to extinguish
what was culturally ours in order
to make it easier to perform

Those who standardly deviated
from the means were shot to
death for failure to conform

We were given an Uncle Tom role
model in an effort to stimulate
Told where we could live, work,
and with whom we could mate

Occasionally, they punished us-
both positive and negative
But there were those among us
who died simply because they
could not find a reason to live

What they wanted to measure
was a relatively permanent change
But to their displeasure
we refused to be tamed
They T-tested us through
their kangaroo courts and again
we proved to be insignificant
despite the behaviors we were taught

So they concluded by calling it
"Territorial-Behavior"-
*People acting strange in a
certain geographical space*

But I'm glad we don't act like they do
I'm so happy that we're abnormal -
You could see it on my face

STRANGE FRUIT

I am a black man but —
I be a black woman too!

"I am as ancient as the world
and older than the flow
of human blood
in human veins

Yes - I've known rivers
Ancient dusty rivers
And my soul has grown deep
Just like the rivers"

Langston wrote about rivers,
which lately, I've come to know
Lady Day sang a prophetic and painful
song about "Strange Fruit" swinging
on a southern tree, ever so slow

Both of them are now gone
but I know what they must have
been thinking when they thought
it was alright to speak about it

Now, if I can just get myself together
you can believe I'm gonna shout it
'Cause I am a black man —
but I be a black woman too!

From the lottery of life
This be the card I drew
Don't attempt to tell me
that I'm somebody
No! not after all that's been done

With much resistance,
I was brought here to suffer
the infirmities of a sick people
who successfully withdrew
my sense of somebody-ness

I am a function of a society
where the blood flows
and the body sway -
where the times change
but the blues stay
I was kidnapped from Africa
where there was no doubt that
I was a warrior
      a Queen or
      a King
Now, like a bird,
I'm caught in a cage
but still I sing
'Cause I am a black man-
but I be a black woman too!

SOME FOLKS ARE THE HARDEST TO DEAL WITH

Some folks are the hardest to deal with;
They really are the most difficult to overcome

I never understood why, in their illusion,
they pretend to be part of the solution
when it's clear — they are the problem

Seldom do they attempt to divorce themselves
                                           from the 60s
They boast of their inclusion
as if the 1960s was a means to an end

They wear the 60s high on their chest
                                      like a metal
A license to say - "see, I was down with the cause.
                                  here's my street cred"

But, their involvement, which never pierced
the surface, doesn't exempt them from what is
still happening

To secure a ride on Freedom's Train,
they stake their claim on the fruit of our labor
They reap what they didn't sow

Some folks really are the hardest to deal with

When push comes to shove,
        they never produce one iota of evidence,
which validates their push -
No scratches, bruises or scars,
                    No broken bones or split homes
                    to state the case
                    No unemployment lines,
        crowded prison or wasted minds
No loss of self-esteem
Tell me, where are the battered wives,
        shattered lives, or brutally beaten children?
                The liquor stores, crack houses, and cheap
                motels

The dropouts
      cop-out
        and crutches.

Where's the evidence they've been in a battle to fit in?

Misfits tend to act like misfits when they don't see how they fit in

Wearing a 60s badge across your chest ain't it -
                                                if you ain't it

Some folks forget what it's like to be hungry
        because someone threw them a crust of bread
        - not you of course

They're drunk with the wine of indifference
        Blinded by the glamour and glare of a
        Hollywood script
They believe they made it by their own boot straps — not you

Some folks are the hardest to deal with — not you

They wear their particular nemesis on their face
Black is such a convenient hue

Instead of coming together,
        we're drifting apart

Nevertheless, the struggle will continue
        and the only hue it respects - is blood red

MILITANT

All things being equal is now
much more out of balance
Both the conditions and the game
rules have drastically changed

It has now hit home

It is no longer a question
No longer taboo to discuss
race and is trickling down effects
If necessity is the mother of invention,
then oppression is the father of motivation

A certain principal person,
otherwise known as the president,
has done us a big favor
For that,
we owe him our gratitude
We must thank God then begin
to do our Go-down-Moses thing

But this time, let's do it right
let my people, the bourgeois ones
who assumed they were living in the Big House
But found out, they were really in the barn

The message is simply this:
When confronted and face with
discrimination and oppression,
if you can't do the principal thing-
then do the righteous thing
If you cannot be drastic,
then begin to turn the wheels
of pragmatism in the motion toward
the ultimate solution for justice -
Be about changing
Be about trying
Be about liberating
But whatever you be
You must be serious —
Brother

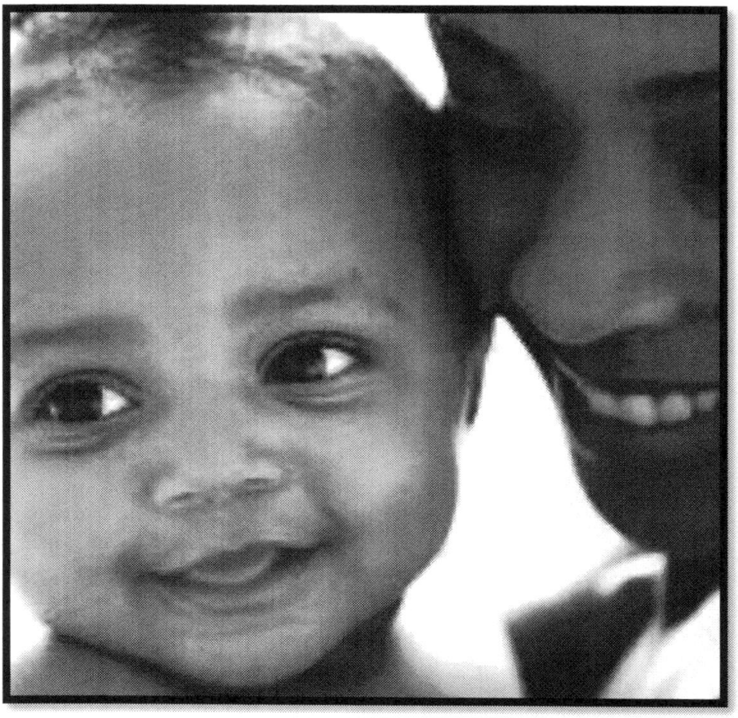

WHATEVER THE TOLL

Let it not be said that a mother bears not the pain of her unborn child while it is yet in her womb

For with every birth pain there is assurance of life in her

And when her unborn is finally born
she instinctively but lovingly secures its needs
-    WHATEVER THE TOLL

It is also true that when her child hungers and is not of age to harvest its own needs the mother naturally and lovingly fulfills the need
-    WHATEVER THE TOLL

In time of illness, a mother feels for her child. She rests not until the sickness subsides

If the illness is long term, she continues to lovingly provide the hope,
for now, hope is needed
-    WHATEVER THE TOLL

When the time her child to enter the marketplace to secure livelihood
If there is no work, let it be known that the mother has set aside for this rainy day
She has done so willingly and lovingly
-    WHATEVER THE TOLL

It is instructive to learn that when trouble causes despair in the heart of the
mother, when her child has been put way - of little consequence is the reason
Her love and support does not wither
And it doesn't waver
-    WHATEVER THE TOLL

When circumstances have allowed
the aging process to set in, and death
of her child draws near, let it be known that
despite her own illness and age, the mother
lives only to cushion the child's pain. She
prays for forgiveness and grace
Her love is everlasting
-   **WHATEVER THE TOLL**

And if love teaches love,
there is no greater love on earth
than a mother's love

In times of sickness, famine,
trouble and death

A MOTHER'S LOVE IS UNCONDITIONAL

A POEM FOR YOU

Thinking that you deserve something nice
and wanting to be concise
A thought popped in my head!
How wonderful it would be to write a few
words that even Shakespeare never said

Words about you and all that you are
Simple words - not too distant, not too far

My thoughts were spearheaded
by your pictures on my wall
My feelings were captivated
with your timely telephone call

I love the way you care
and praise your every breath
I'm so into you that
there's little of me left

There's really no way to explain
how nice it is to feel
So good about a person
Someone who is so real

It reassures the body
and stimulates the mind
Just to be linked in love
with someone of your kind
How marvelous a thought
that brings joy along
To encounter a melody
and put it in a song

It makes me shout out loud
Sing happy with glee
Dance up and down so proud,
knowing, yes - you love me

I can't predict our future
and all that we will do
But on this day, I desired
To tell you that I love you
So I wrote a poem for you

DREAM ENCOUNTER

The face of my dream can see with 10 eyes
Yet, it hears with less than an ear
It has a sound mind but a head unclear

As I began to pursue my dream,
there were 9 obstacles
obstructing me - seeking to alter my course
But my will was just too strong.
It blew them away with righteousness
and a mighty force

Eight times I had to fight the foe of those who criticized
Unbelievers were telling me to turn back and
demon were dressed in a most clever disguise

Seven years of bad luck would not change one of my ideas.
Six high mountains and low valleys managed to slow me
down but my spirit was moving somewhere

I encountered five hard feelings from five dear
friends, which left a bitter taste in my mouth

Four more setbacks staggered me a bit
As I started out, I never contemplated it

3° below zero was cold enough to freeze a running stream.
Cold enough to freeze my body but not my dream

The dream seemed to fuel my drive and urge my soul
to press on. It gave me the warmth I needed and
made me twice as strong

When I finally reached my promise land
there was yet one thing that I had to do

Think about where I had come from and
understand that I was not quite through

SIMPLE SCIENCE

In an era where so many have grown accustomed to instant coffee, quick grits and ready-made biscuits, there is such a thing as over doing it. Ever since they split the DNA, invented the Apple Computer and set foot on the moon, some have come to accept science as a means to all ends.

Newsflash! They caught Willie the bank robber the other day. This would not be news except for the scientific lessons, which were about to be learned. Had it not been for what was perceived to be, "in the interest of science" by a few hyped-up, over-zealous social researchers, Willie would have been quickly tried and sentenced for his crimes.

Having only a fourth-grade education and being a product of a broken family, under most circumstances, would not have qualified Willie for such an important role. However, what was unique and surprising about Willie, was the fact that in a 20 year period, he managed to elude federal, state and local authorities and rob over 200 banks.

"How is that possible?" cried one police authority.

"Where did he get the expertise?" replied another.

Still, another official saw Willie's capture as a unique opportunity to study the criminal mind. "Perhaps we can unlock the mystery of the age-old question, what makes the criminal mind function?" they mused. They began to brainstorm more questions – "What's behind the drive for anti-social, maladaptive behavior?" "Why do they do it?"

"Ah," replied one of them. "Those people are all criminals. It's in their nature. Perhaps it's their broken homes - who knows? Who cares?"

"I think we should really find out" said one official. "

I do to," agreed another.

"Good! Let's arrange for a case study on his family."

When the study was completed, they did not find anything radically different in Willie's family's history than any other poor barely literate family.

So next, they surgically opened, weighed and studied Willie's brain before reattaching his skull. After carefully analyzing his brain structure, rhythms and patterns, they found nothing abnormal about its size, shape or functions.

Finally, as a last resort, one of the clinical researchers received a brainstorm of his own.

"Why don't we simply ask him when he's cross-examined at the trial?"

They alerted the judge to their intentions and of course, "in the interest of science," the judge agreed. In fact, the judge was so excited about their little social experiment on criminal behavior, that he summoned the local newspaper who leaked their intentions to the national media.

Pretty soon, it was the talk of the town. Willie's trail was now an event; a- who's who among celebrities. Everybody, who was anybody, simply had to attend. Beautiful people from all over the country jammed into the tiny courtroom while others viewed the event from their living rooms or local bars.

Finally, the day of the trial arrived. The bailiff hustled Willie into the court room with his hands tightly cuffed behind his back, sat him down in the chair, and swore him into the court.

"Now Willie," said one of the esteemed researchers.

"We've had an opportunity to review your entire family's history. We've studied your anatomy from your blood type to the actual weight of your brain. We've looked into the environment that you were raised and attempted to duplicate the conditions as best we could. Yet, we still don't know what makes you tick.

We know you're a product of a broken home. And we know that you barely completed the fourth-grade. What we don't know is the science behind the intricacies and nuances of the criminal mind.

In this court room today, we've assembled some of the finest clinical scientists and social researchers in the country. Willie, we'd like you, in your own words, right here in front of them, to answer this one little question."

"Why do you rob so many banks?"

Willie glared into the court room, the television cameras and the hundreds of faces who had gathered for this momentous occasion. He smiled and casually replied in a low voice,

"Because that's where the money is!"

Stolen Lives
KILLED BY LAW ENFORCEMENT

RUNNING IN THE NIGHT

If there was a reason for the incident, it wasn't revealed. Nevertheless, it was news. Everywhere I went, people were talking about it. The entire community was shaken.

At first, I thought the mob, which had gathered around Sam's Candy store, was a-waiting to see what the daily number would be. But soon it was clear to me that they were not. From my third-floor window, I could hear their emotion and bitterness. I could hear Sam's voice the most,

"Damn shame, gotdamn shame. They didn't have to do it."

I heard another voice say,

"I know his family; they good people. Dammit! It didn't have to go down like this? Who's going to pay for this?"

Yet another voice cried,

"It all happened so fast. One minute, I saw him dashing down the street, the next thing I know; they had 'em."

On the streets, where the talk was loud, on the corner, where the sideshows prevailed, there was nothing new, nothing at all. People were shouting, "We are to do something." Though I felt their pains and was sorry about the shooting, I did not offer a word. For a brief moment, we were unified in our rage, but I knew it wouldn't last. Instantly, my mind raced back to at least three other incidents in the past decade. I kept trying to connect all them to something Brother Malcolm said years before.

I reflected on the many people who gave their lives in the struggle. Perhaps my thoughts were obsolete. Perhaps they were better suited for the classroom. It seems that when all of talk dies down, no one will be talking about it anymore. There was no forum for it. It would no longer be fashionable to discuss it in the barbershop or beauty parlor. The media wouldn't touch it. How long could anyone be expected to carry hatred in their hearts?

If we, the community, agreed on any one thing, we could never agree on two. Were we, as a people, capable of regenerating the spirit, which prevailed like an eternal flame during the 1960s or had we become too complacent? In my view, we never really went all the way. There was always something or someone to dampen the flames of protest.

When we summoned community meetings, people like Mrs. Green would never attend. Her excuse was she had four kids to look after. Johnny G on the fifth floor could not go along with holding back rent until management provided security cameras. Even Sam, the merchant, backed away from our plan to boycotting certain stores, which were known drug havens. I wonder why?

I took a hard look at the system and saw it for what it was - full of loopholes for many to dodge their way through it. The politicians seemed to dodge the best. One case in point was this incident. This was not an election year so no self-respecting politician wanted to tackle the problem. Politicians had a way of only showing up in an election year. If this was an election year, I'm sure they would've knocked on my door. Perhaps then, I could properly introduce them to my urban conditions. They could formally meet the rats and roaches that occupy my dwellings. Perhaps they could shake hands and kiss their offspring.

If this was an election year, the Eyewitness-News would have allotted more coverage to the incident than seven seconds. If the shoe was on the other foot, if the perpetrator was the victim, there would've been more coverage, more outcries. But, this was not an election year.

Still, I felt it was our responsibility to highlight these incidents of injustice, not the politicians or the media. It was time we started taking control of our own community just like every other community does. In the 60s, in this same community, an incident like this never went unaddressed. I will admit we sometimes we went about doing it the wrong way, but we acted.

We staged sit-ins and boycotts and formed community watch groups. Operating on the premise, that the squeaky wheel gets the oil, names like Malcolm, Martin, Angela, George, Jackie, Roy, and Fanny Lou became our heroes. But I feel today's youth have forgotten who paved the way for them.

Of course, this wasn't the 60s, this was the 80s. The 60s seemed light- years away. For that matter, so did the lessons I learned in grammar school. I learned every sentence needed two parts to make sense - a subject and a verb. But I cannot give yesterday's Daily News a passing grade for good grammar because on page 32 their headline read, 'A Man Shot Running in the Night'. It failed to give a reason or rationale for his death. It failed to make sense. He committed no crime, no gang warfare - no explanation for his death whatsoever.

Yesterday evening
around a quarter past ten
a boy was shot down,
shot down before his life began
The story went on to say
at last report
he was not dead
but what chance did he have
surviving a bullet to the head

Some say it was murder
perhaps in the first-degree
premeditated by the po-po
in an effort
to clean up the community

But we who knew the boy
can really state his case
he never harmed anybody;
his death was a disgrace

Every once in a while
a brother gets shot
for no particular reason
Hunted down by the police
like an animal, as if

it was open season

On the streets we better wake up
before there's any more
                    bloodshed
We'd better open our eyes
                    to what's happening
            and try to remember
                    what brother Malcolm said

It's a shame that it takes tragedy
For something like this to come to light
The boy never harmed anyone.
His only crime was running in the night

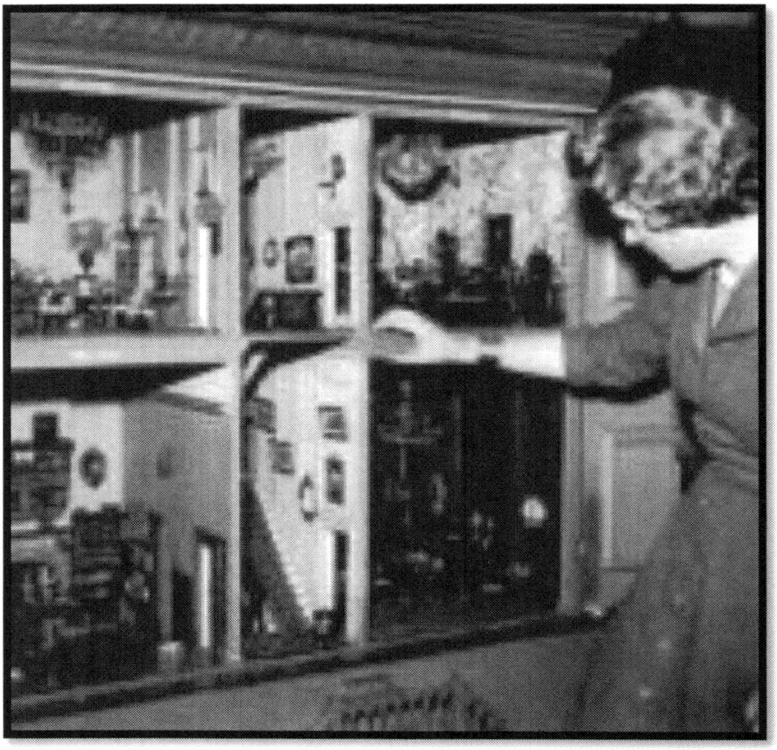

DREAM HOUSE

By Linda Wright

As a child, I was extremely partial to all types of doll houses, would often visit various shops displaying anything of the sort. I promised myself one day I would own one of my own. As I matured, instead of growing out of my desire, I grew into it and developed what was almost an obsession.

I searched constantly for the one house made just for me, much as one would search for a home to live in. I even considered building one of my own but finally admitted to myself I wouldn't be able to create what I was longing for.

On one extremely stormy day, I was running to the bus stop with a newspaper over my head. Unfortunately, I wasn't fast enough and the bus pulled off with a roar. I glared angrily after it and had to enter a nearby shop for shelter. It was in this dingy old place that I finally found my dream house.

It was absolutely beautiful. I stared in disbelief at this perfect specimen and anxiously search for the proprietor who was somewhere in the back room of the store. He was an old man, very old, with stooped shoulders and a fringe of gray here encircling his scalp. Balancing precariously on his bulbous nose was a pair of pince-nez. His suspenders did a poor job of holding up his pants. But to me, he was the most fabulous sight to behold, for in his possession was the one thing I was lacking.

After a short time, which was spent haggling over a fair price, we agreed on the cost of $500. Unbeknownst to the salesman, I would have agreed to any price he concocted and I was quite delirious with elation as he carefully packed the miniature house and all of the tiny accessories. As I left, I glanced at the man and he seemed to be smiling strangely . . .

I decided to take a cab so that no clumsy oaf would cause me to drop my joy on the crowded bus, along with the fact that my treasure was weighty. I obviously had an inane look on my face, as the cabbie was looking at me in the rear view mirror and shaking his head in amusement.

Arriving home twenty minutes later, I tip the driver generously. He looked at the $20 bill in astonishment and leaped to my assistance in transporting my goods inside my apartment.

Forgetting all of the responsibilities, I buried myself in the tedious task of arranging the miniature furnishings, appraising each separately. What joy there was therein. Oil paintings, a piano ("It really plays!" I exclaimed). The chandelier was genuine French crystal and tinkled merrily at the slightest breeze. The carpet was deeply plush and colored a deep wine. There was a fireplace, a spiral staircase and other beautiful features, too numerous to describe. The house was fully electrified and sported running water also. There was a family of life-like dolls, the parents and two children, a boy and a girl and a beautiful St. Bernard dog. I was more than pleased.

Nothing would do except for the house to be displayed in my sitting room so that I could boast it at every opportunity. It took hours of arranging and rearranging the furnishings before I finally became tired enough to call it a night.

I must've been asleep an hour or so when something awakened me. I seemed to hear, no, I did hear noises from the sitting room. I hastily arose and armed myself and moved noiselessly down the hall. What my eyes beheld at the portal to this room was not to be believed and I stood rooted to the spot with my mouth gaping in astonishment.

Every light in the little house was ablaze and there was movement and many sounds emitting from within. I watched, fascinated, as the dolls went about everyday routines, as any normal family would. The children were watching television, the father was lounging beside the fireplace which was burning brightly, reading a newspaper. Most amazing was the mother, busily preparing a meal and I

could actually smell the delicious aromas wafting from within. I moved closer to this phenomenon and I obviously distracted the father from his relaxation for he started quickly from his chair to face me. I could see many emotions crossing his face until one of resignation, then determination, stamped itself there. It was then that he spoke to me.

"You are the first owner I have ever had the pleasure of meeting. All of the others ran from us in fear and quickly returned us to the little shop we were in. It has been a long while since we were last purchased. Allow me to introduce myself. I have acquired the name of Jonathan Redgrave, the others are my wife, Ingrid, and my children, John Jr. and Allison. We are here by the grace and power of God, for with His everlasting love, He gave us this semblance of life.

We were a God-fearing family in our true life. We loved each other and praised the Lord in our hearts and minds. Life was good to us. We were blessed with beauty and love in this world.

"One night, while we lay dreaming in our beds, the boiler exploded in our basement and we were killed in the flames. St. Peter deigned to find some way to repay us our pureness of heart so we came to life again in this manner. We have been this way for over 20 years.

"All of our previous owners were afraid of us. In their eyes, we were demons, or haunts, but in truth, we are angels from Heaven. And if you suffer us to abide in your home, you will surely be blessed; yes, you and all that you own."

After this touching monologue, my love for the house, and the little people within, grew. I bowed my head in reverence and bid them good night. In the mornings, I, of course, thought this was an imaginative dream stemming from my love for the house. I laughed at my reverie as I donned my clothes.

Before I left the house, I had to take one last look at my treasure. The father was still in the chair and I smiled to myself. But wait, did he just wink at me? No - it just couldn't be!! Then, I ran for my bus, to another day at work.